Final Fantasy The Play: Invasion

THOMAS EMMETT

Copyright © 2021 Thomas Emmett

All rights reserved.

ISBN: 9798642353646

Look for this book and more on my author page at:
https://www.amazon.com/author/thomasemmett

CONTENTS

Act	Title	Page
Extra:	Main Characters	1
Act 1:	Aftermath	7
Act 2:	The Nautilus	31
Act 3:	Sneaking In	57
Act 4:	The Rescue	85
Act 5:	The Protector	118
Extra:	World Maps	154

Final Fantasy The Play Book List

1. The Birth of a Legend
2. The Time Krystal
3. The Past Returns
4. Chocobo Island
5. Secret of Lindsea
6. Invasion

Main Characters

Name: Thomas Armet

Hometown: Karnak

Description: 21 year old white male. 5 foot 10. Moderate tan. Moderate muscle. Little fat. Medium length, light brown hair. Green eyes.

Class: Fighter.

Outfit: Dark blue pants, dark blue short sleeve shirt, black belt, black boots, black sword sheath on back.

Weapons: Long sword, dagger.

Story: A young man who witnessed the death of his parents when he was little. He has spent his whole life in different parts of the Western Continent. He was a slave, a gladiator, and a prisoner at one point. Despite his rough past, he is mentioned in several prophecies as being very important when it comes to saving the planet. His motivation and goal in life is to kill the ones responsible for the death of his parents.

Name: Dustin Helios

Hometown: Windy Village

Description: 27 year old white male. 6 foot 8. Dark tan. Lot of muscle. Moderate fat. Short dark brown hair. Brown eyes.

Class: Gladiator.

Outfit: Torn brown shorts, brown short sleeve shirt, black belt, black boots, black sword and axe sheath on back.

Weapons: Double sided axe, long sword.

Story: A young man who also suffered through the death of his father when he was little. He has spent his life trying to find work, and a purpose in living. He and Thomas are cousins, and together they seek to restore the throne which was stolen from them. His great size and strength prove useful in a tight spot.

Name: Cid Highwind

Hometown: Timber Village

Description: 22 year old white male. 6 foot 1. Light tan. Little muscle. Little fat. Medium length, light brown hair. Brown eyes.

Class: Archer.

Outfit: Dark red pants, white long sleeve shirt, brown belt, brown boots, dark red hat, brown arrow quiver on back.

Weapons: Long bow, dagger.

Story: A young man who desperately seeks to prove himself to the world with his archery skills. He exhibits a tough exterior, but deep down he feels alone, and uncertain. He witnessed the disappearance of his best friend in the past, yet he still continues to search for her. Despite his best efforts, he continues to lose hope that he will ever find her again.

Name: Amanda Hancock

Hometown: Wutai

Description: 20 year old white female. 5 foot 2. Light tan. Little muscle. Little fat. Shoulder length black hair. Brown eyes.

Class: Thief.

Outfit: Black pants, black short sleeve shirt, black belt, black shoes, black hooded cape, two black dagger sheaths in belt.

Weapons: Two daggers.

Story: A young, misunderstood woman. She is both well known, and wanted, throughout both of the major kingdoms for her life of thievery. She suffered the death of both of her parents recently, though her current motivations are unknown. She can put on quite a show, and is easily underestimated. Those who do, however, will quickly meet their demise.

Name: Mary Conway

Hometown: Lindsea

Description: 20 year old white female. 5 foot 5. Light tan. Little muscle. Little fat. Blonde hair down to middle of the back. Blue eyes.

Class: White mage.

Outfit: Pink short sleeve dress to the knees, dark pink short coat with short sleeves that covers chest and ribs, dark pink shoes.

Weapons: Short staff.

Story: The young princess of Lindsea. She lost her father before she was born, and was raised by her mother. She is highly educated, though she has never left the safety of the castle until now. She desperately wants to do what is right, but lacks confidence in herself. Her magic knowledge and abilities will prove quite useful over time.

Act 1: AFTERMATH

Scene 1: Lindsea Castle

(Setting: The aftermath of the battle for Lindsea. The background is filled with smoke, fire, and destruction. The castle is still mainly intact, but a lot of the walls are broken, or crumbling. Horses, soldiers, and siege equipment are all over the place. The Stephis army has escaped, and are making their way back to the Western Continent. The remaining Lindsea soldiers are trying to restore peace, and order. They are currently spread out throughout the castle, and the town. The townsfolk are also out, and are trying to assist as well. This scene begins where the last one ended. Thomas and Galahad are searching through the rubble outside the castle. With the rest of the party off to deliver the white Master Krystal to Merlin, Thomas is trying desperately to get back inside the collapsed tunnel. It is currently bright and sunny outside.)

Thomas: (Frustrated.) "I can't find a way in! We have to get Mary out of there!"

Galahad: (Tries to calm Thomas down.) "I know you're upset. I want to find to her too. But this mess here... It will take a lot of man power to clear all this away."

Thomas: (Picks up a large stone, and heaves it away.) "I won't give up on her!"

Galahad: (Stops to think.) "Maybe we are going about this the wrong way."

Thomas: "What do you mean? It's simple. We find Mary, and get her out of there."

Galahad: "I mean, maybe we can't get in this way. There has to be another entrance somewhere. With all the explosions and blasts around, surely there is another way into the tunnel. After all, Nichols and the others were able to get inside. They probably also already found a way out. We should move from this spot, and see what else we can find."

Thomas: "You're right. They certainly didn't just walk in the front door like we did. If that was the only normal way in, then they must have made their own way in someplace else. Hopefully that entrance isn't destroyed now as well."

(Thomas and Galahad aren't sure which direction to start looking in, so they head back towards the main keep. There are soldiers and rubble all over the place. They have to carefully make their way through all the activity.)

Galahad: "We should check on the queen as well, and tell her the news."

Thomas: "You think she might know another way in?"

Galahad: "I don't know. But if she is still in the throne room, she may have seen them enter the tunnels from above. You can see a lot from up there."

Thomas: "Then let's go there first. We might even be able to spot an opening."

(Galahad leads the way to the keep, and up to the queen's throne room. Thomas is saddened to see the current condition of the castle, but he knows that Lindsea will be able to repair itself over time. His only goal now is to find Mary. The two finally reach the throne room, and find it in nearly perfect condition. The throne, the carpet, and even all the pots of roses are still in place. They spot the queen standing near the window, and make their way over.)

Galahad: (Bows.) "Highness."

Rose: "You have returned. Where are all the others? And Mary?"

Galahad: "It was Nichols. He was here. They found a way to get inside the tunnels. We all fought well, but he had cast a very powerful spell, and it caused the tunnels to collapse. The others were able to move the white Krystal to safety. I stayed behind with Thomas. Mary is missing, majesty. We are making haste to find her."

Rose: "The reserves had arrived just in time, and had driven off the invaders. The castle should be clear now. Find Mary, and report back to me."

Thomas: "Did you see anything from up here? Did you see how they got inside?"

Rose: "Stephis soldiers came from all over. They marched through the town, then surrounded the castle. After that, they pushed their way in."

Thomas: "Any ideas?"

Galahad: "Let us try the same path. We can start outside the castle walls, circle around, and then make our way inside. We will find the opening."

Thomas: "Ok. Let's get moving."

Scene 2: Merlin's Cave

(Setting: At the entrance to Merlin's cave, inside an old forest. The weather is chilly this afternoon. Clouds fill the sky, and the tall trees block the sun. There is a light rain at the moment. The forest is quiet and empty, aside from the sound of rain falling. There is ice outside the cave entrance, where small waterfalls had previously frozen, but has yet to melt. The party arrives outside the cave with the chocobos pulling the cart. They unhook it, and prepare to pull the cart with the white Krystal into the cave. Amanda secures the chocobos to some trees before they continue.)

Dustin: "That was much easier than the last trip here. The chocobos can move the Krystal like it's nothing."

Cid: "They are very helpful."

(Cid, Amanda, and Dustin begin the trip inside the cave. They eventually enter the Krystal room, and find Merlin examining the red Master Krystal. He turns around to see them pulling the white Krystal through the door.)

Merlin: (Smiling.) "My! Is that what I think it is?"

Amanda: "You bet it is! The white Master Krystal. We rescued it out of Lindsea."

Merlin: (Walks over to the cart.) "That must have been some trip."

Dustin: "This one wasn't so bad. The chocobos made it much easier."

Merlin: "Chocobos? Are you sure?"

Amanda: "Yep. We each have one. We found them on the island."

Merlin: "I can see we have some catching up to do. Where are the others? Thomas? Mary?"

Cid: "About that..."

Dustin: "We were separated during the battle. Thomas stayed behind to look for Mary, while we got the Krystal out. We really should get back over there."

Merlin: "I heard about Stephis attacking the kingdom. Your moogle friends told me."

Dustin: (While releasing the Krystal.) "They made it?"

Merlin: "Yes indeed. They have actually been quite helpful around here. It seems they have decided to stay. They have been assisting me to prepare better sleeping conditions, and they have even helped set up a stable for the animals. You should be able to bring your chocobos inside now to keep them safe."

Cid: "I think after we get this Krystal in place we should be going back. Things weren't looking so good when we left."

Amanda: "It should be fine if we stay the night. Not like we have been able to rest much anyway lately. It's almost dark as it is."

Cid: "I know you're right. We do need to sleep, even if it's just a little."

Merlin: "Come now. Let us set up the Krystal, bring in your rides, and then we can work on something to eat and drink while we catch up. The moogles are around here somewhere. I'm sure they will be glad to see you."

(The four of them move the Krystal from the cart to where the other two are in the room. They set it up in position, and examine their work.)

Merlin: "So where did you find this one, exactly?"

Cid: "It was in the underground tunnels beneath Lindsea. As we had suspected. At first we were just there to protect it, but when the whole place fell apart, we decided it was safer to move. Nichols showed up with some new spell, along with a bunch of monster soldiers, and the tunnels were destroyed."

Merlin: "Unbelievable."

Amanda: (Looking at the Krystals.) "They do look really good together. Green, red, and white. All we have left to find are the blue and the black. And we know where the black one is."

Dustin: "Am I the only one here that is slightly concerned about keeping them all in one place?"

Merlin: "It is a risk. But every place has its risks. This is in my mind one of the safest places in the world. Which is why I am here, and not elsewhere."

Amanda: "Hey, Cid! Let's go bring them in already."

Cid: "Ok. We'll be back."

(Amanda and Cid head back outside to fetch the three chocobos to bring them in. Dustin meets up with Mogmatt and Mogsara in the cave, and takes a tour of the new changes. While he waits, Merlin checks over the white Krystal. When the chocobos arrive, the moogles take them to the stables to get them ready for the night, while everyone else gathers in the Krystal room. Dustin decides to give Amanda and Cid a quick tour before dinner.)

Dustin: (Attempts to sound like a tour guide.) "The cave is a bit different than you remember it. Please, allow me to show you to your quarters."

Amanda: "Just make it snappy, mister. I'm famished!"

Scene 3: Lindsea Castle

(Setting: Thomas and Galahad are in a small boat, and are circling the outer wall of the castle in the moat. They have been searching everywhere, but have yet to find Mary, or Nichols. They are beginning to lose hope, but are determined to stick to the plan, and search the entire area. Rubble, and the remains of battle, are everywhere. Clouds fill the sky now, with a light rain coming down. Thomas and Galahad take turns with the paddles as they circle the castle. They are nearly to the back section, half way around the wall. They have come across some unmanned boats floating around, but nothing else unusual.)

Thomas: (Switches spots with Galahad.) "Let me look around while you row for a while. I have a strange feeling that we aren't alone anymore."

Galahad: "If we only had Mary's key, we could have probably just went inside the tunnels through the door. Unfortunately, we have no way of knowing if the entire path is still clear."

Thomas: "And we would have to deal with the undead by ourselves. That's if we could even get to the door. Remember we tried to get back out, but something was blocking it?"

Galahad: "Oh yes. That is correct. Looks like this is the only way left."

(Galahad continues to row while Thomas checks the area. Most of the walls here seem to be intact. The wind and rain starts to pick up, making small waves in the water. It also makes it harder to see.)

Galahad: "Anything?"

Thomas: "I can't hear much over this rain. But I think I see something over there. Keep rowing!"

(The boat continues through the water, until they both spot what appears to be a hole in the wall. Galahad rows the boat toward it, and Thomas hops out to tie the boat to a small tree.)

Thomas: "I'm pretty sure this isn't a normal part of the wall."

Galahad: (Climbs out of the boat, and joins Thomas on the

muddy bank.) "Certainly not." (Examines the hole.) "It's messy. Like someone blew it open. I'd say a man could fit inside here."

Thomas: "Let's go inside, and see where it leads."

(Thomas and Galahad squeeze through the hole one at a time. Once they are through, the space opens up some more. It kind of looks like the tunnels, but there's a ton of dirt and loose rocks here.)

Thomas: (Finds a barely lit torch on the wall, and takes it.) "Someone came this way. We should keep going. See if there is more light up ahead."

Galahad: (Finds another torch, and removes it from the holder.) "This should help."

(They continue through the dirt and stone passageway. The temperature drops slightly as they go, despite the burning torches on the walls. They find various weapons and pieces of armor along the way on the ground, but nothing really useful.)

Galahad: (Picks up a gauntlet.) "Looks like Stephis to me. This has to be how they got in."

(They continue a little more, and are suddenly faced with three Stephis soldiers limping toward them in the distance. The two groups spot each other, and draw their weapons.)

Galahad: "Stragglers. Maybe they know where Mary is."

Thomas: "Yeah. We should go ask them."

(The two groups move toward each other, and prepare to fight. The soldiers seem injured, and much less willing, but they quickly reveal their monster forms.)

Thomas: (Takes a look at the bandersnatch, the ahriman, and the bite bug. He is quite ready to attack with his sword, but pauses.) "Where's Mary?"

Bite Bug: "Mary who?"

Bandersnatch: "You actually think we would tell you anything?"

Galahad: "Maybe you won't talk to us, but you will talk."

Bandersnatch: "We'll see about that."

Galahad: "Thomas! We need to take one alive. We can interrogate him in the dungeon. Find out where Mary is."

Thomas: "Well I've made my choice."

(Thomas slices the bite bug, who falls to the ground. Galahad finishes him off with a second blow of his sword. Thomas turns to the ahriman, but the bandersnatch cuts him up with his claws. Galahad manages to get a hit on the ahriman, and Thomas is able to finish him off with a second.)

Thomas: "You're coming with us!"

Bandersnatch: "I'm not afraid of you!"

Galahad: "You will be when Lancelot is done with you!"

(The bandersnatch manages to bite Galahad, but Thomas attacks with his sword. Galahad follows with a second hit, and Thomas gets another dose of the claws. Galahad gets a final cut in on the beast, who then falls to the ground.)

Galahad: "Now he's down. We can take him back to the castle for interrogation. We'll see how much he knows."

Thomas: "Yeah! It's about time we get some answers here."

Scene 4: Lindsea Castle

(Setting: The throne room of Queen Rose, on the top floor of Lindsea Castle. The queen is sitting on her throne at the far end of the room. On either side of her is a great window overlooking the town. A long red carpet stretches from her throne to the doorway, where two guards stand by. The queen is wearing a red dress, red shoes, and a small gold crown. The room is full of potted rose bushes of multiple colors. A servant is seen watering each pot. It is day time, and the light from the outside is keeping the room bright. The party has returned to Lindsea, and is coming to meet with the queen. Cid walks up to Rose while Dustin and Amanda follows.)

Cid: (Bows.) "We have returned, majesty."

Rose: "Wonderful! I've been expecting you. Is the white Krystal safe?"

Cid: "It is. Stephis will not be able to find it now."

Rose: "Excellent. We have much to catch up on. Are you aware that Mary is still missing?"

Dustin: "She was missing when we left with the Krystal, and Thomas and Galahad went off to find her. Have they not found her yet?"

Rose: "No. I am afraid not."

Amanda: "Then what are we waiting for? Let's get moving!"

Rose: (Holds up her hand.) "Wait! Before you go, you must hear me. While you were gone, Thomas and Galahad searched the entire castle, and found the place where Stephis had entered the tunnels. They went inside to investigate, and came across some stragglers from Stephis. They managed to capture one of them, and took him to the dungeon. General Lancelot is currently interrogating the prisoner as we speak. He is attempting to learn as much as he can, and hopefully find out what happened to Mary. Thomas said that the prisoner seemed to know about her at first, but he was unwilling to talk. Lucky for us, Lancelot has certain persuasive abilities that may prove useful here."

Dustin: "Where is Thomas now?"

Rose: "He's downstairs. In the dungeon."

Cid: "And Galahad?"

Rose: "He is currently working on some other important tasks for me. You may head down to the dungeon if you wish. I will have one of my guards escort you there. I'm sure Thomas will be glad to see you again."

Cid: (Bows.) "Thank you."

~~~~~~~~~~

A little later... in the dungeon...

Amanda: (Looks around.) "Wow! This must be the creepiest place in all Lindsea."

Dustin: "It definitely doesn't look like it belongs here."

(The three make their way through the dark and damp underground. Flaming torches line the stones walls of the dungeon, while water drips in random locations. There are several cells built into the walls on both sides of the hallway. The party peers inside each one as they walk past, and finds a few prisoners that are locked up. Most of them seem to be sleeping. They continue to the end of the hall, where they find a large wooden door. Dustin pushes it open, and they enter a new room. They find Thomas sitting alone at a small wooden table, and another closed door on the opposite end of the room.)

Dustin: "There you are!"

Thomas: (Turns around to look, then stands up.) "Boy am I glad to see you guys!"

(Thomas hugs each one of them, then has each person sit around the table with him. A lone lantern glows on the top of it.)

Thomas: "How is the white Krystal? Is it safe with Merlin?"

Amanda: "Yep. Merlin and the moogles."

Thomas: "That's great. It really is. It's always nice to hear when something goes right."

Cid: "What's going on here? What did we miss?"

Thomas: "We couldn't find Mary anywhere. We looked all over. The only thing we did find were a few leftover soldiers from Stephis. We were able to capture the one, and Lancelot is in there trying to make him talk. He seemed pretty determined not to though."

(The party stops when they hear a scream. It sounds like it came from the other side of the door.)

Amanda: "I think he might be making some progress."

Thomas: "Anyway, I'm just waiting for the moment. I really don't know what else to do until we get something. Lancelot has been at it for a while now."

Cid: "I know this must be hard for you. It's hard for all of us."

Dustin: "Is there anything we can do for you? Want me to find some Stephis soldiers for you to pound on?"

Thomas: "I don't think so. I just want to find Mary."

Amanda: (Pulls out her daggers, and starts cutting at the air.) "You think Lancelot needs some back up in there? I'll make him talk. Make him tell me all he knows."

(The party stops again as they hear a series of loud bangs. They look all over, but it seems to be coming from behind the door.)

Cid: "What are they doing in there?"

Dustin: "I wonder if he's ok. Lancelot might need our help."

Thomas: "We took real good care of the bandersnatch. He didn't have anything left when we were done with him. I don't see him being able to hurt anyone right now."

(Suddenly, the closed door slowly creaks open. The party stands up, and pulls out their weapons. As they prepare to fight, they watch an armored Lancelot walk through the door, and shut it behind him. He looks at the group.)

Lancelot: "I see you've all returned. I regret to inform you that the monster is now dead."

Amanda: "Dead?!"

Lancelot: (Smiles.) "But not before he told me everything."

Scene 5: The Mountains

(Setting: A cool, but sunny day. In the mountains on the Western Continent to the east of Stephis. A small group of Stephis soldiers are making their way back from Lindsea. Most of the army has already returned except for this group. The soldiers have been marching and sailing ever since the battle. They are tired, and many are injured. They left most of their equipment behind, and are only carrying their weapons and armor. They are bringing a few prisoners with them who have chains around their necks and hands to prevent escape. Four of the soldiers are carrying a small cage, which is held up in the air by two long poles. Princess Mary sits alone inside the cage. Everyone marches quietly along, the only sounds being the clanging of arms and armor. Princess Mary finally looks up. She squints through the sunlight, and the spaces in the cage. She looks in the distance, and immediately knows where she is.)

Mary: "Stephis. They are taking me back to the castle."

Guard 1: (Turns to Mary.) "Quiet, you! There'll be no words from the prisoners."

Guard 2: "Yeah!"

(Mary returns to sitting there quietly, bouncing up and down as the soldiers walk over the rocky ground. She sighs.)

Guard 1: "I said quiet!"

(Mary checks out the soldiers as they go. They are clearly worn out, but they are determined to get back to the castle. She knows that she would be glad to go back home as well. That is if there even is a home left to go back to. She was taken away so quickly that she didn't even get to see what was going on outside the Lindsea tunnels. She doesn't even know if Thomas and the others are alive, or if the Krystal is safe. She once again feels defeated, and the closer they get to Stephis, the more she wonders if she will ever see Lindsea again.)

Guard 1: "Halt!"

(Mary watches nervously as the guards attempt to work their way through a rough patch of rocks and stones. These mountains are rather dangerous, but everyone has made it through so far. She has been afraid ever since the beginning that they would drop the cage, but luckily that hasn't happened yet. She would almost rather be in the castle on solid ground than to be swinging from side to side in the air. She of course knows that after the mountains comes the swamps, and those will only be slightly easier. But after that, it will likely be the dungeon for her. She just hopes she doesn't run into Nichols again. Not after dealing with all his monster soldiers. She wonders if Nichols even knows she was captured. She lost track of him too after the blast.)

Guard 1: "Ok, everyone. It's time for a break."

(The four guards find a smooth section of dirt, and lower the cage with the poles. They join with the other soldiers in sitting down while they eat and drink a little. Everyone is tired, but the break seems to help. They are still determined to make it back to the castle before dark. Nobody offers any of the prisoners anything to eat or drink, and they all look at the soldiers hoping they might get something. One soldier finally tosses the last of his meal toward the prisoners, and they attempt to divide it amongst themselves. Nobody shares anything with Mary, but they aren't able to see clearly enough into the cage to know who is inside.)

Guard 1: (Stands up again.) "Back to work."

(The four guards grab the poles, and lift the cage back on their shoulders. Mary sways back and forth as the march continues. She hopes they do make it to the castle before night. At least she will be able to have something to eat and drink there. She knows the soldiers can only carry so much, and they are at the end of their supplies, or else they might actually give her some. As she checks ahead, she notices the northwest tower in the distance, and recalls the day when she first met the party.)

Mary: (Thinks to herself.) "That's where everything started. The day everyone broke in, and rescued me. The day we started on our journey. The day I first met Thomas."

(Mary starts to cry as she pictures each of the party members in her mind. She recalls their names, their faces, their individual personalities. All the good times they have had. All the fun, and adventure. And of course the danger. She cries even more when she realizes how much she misses them. But she knows in her heart that she misses one more than all the others. She grabs on to the moonstone pendant around her neck as she thinks of him.)

Mary: "Thomas..."

Act 2: THE NAUTILUS

Scene 1: Lindsea Harbor

(Setting: The coast to the north of Lindsea. There is a small wooden dock where the Lindsea army's ships gather. Soldiers are seen moving to and from the ships. The blue ocean waves are crashing into the dock, causing the boats to bounce around in the water. There isn't much activity at this time since most of the Lindsea soldiers are still at the castle area, but there are some coming and going. It is sunny out, and very windy. A few boats are sailing out in the ocean at the moment. The party is seen making their way toward the dock through the grassy plains as the scene begins.)

Dustin: (Checks out the ships.) "How do we know which one we are looking for?"

Amanda: "Lancelot said it would be a smaller ship."

Cid: (Quickly scans them all.) "But they are all small!"

Thomas: "I don't think this needs to be difficult. Let's just ask someone. I've still got the letter if we need it."

(Two of the Lindsea soldiers notice the party as they reach the dock. They recognize that they aren't dressed in Lindsea armor, and quickly approach them.)

Soldier 1: "Halt! This area is off limits to civilians! What business do you have here?"

Thomas: "We have come on official Lindsea business. We have need of a ship."

Soldier 2: "Have you now? And what sort of business would this be?"

Thomas: (Hands him the letter.) "This letter was written by General Lancelot, and signed by the queen."

Soldier 2: (Takes the letter, and opens it up. He begins to read it quietly.) "It is official. But I don't understand."

Soldier 1: (Takes the letter, and reads it.) "Yes. This is the queen's royal seal." (Looks up at Thomas.) "But this mission of yours... is this serious?"

Thomas: "As serious as we are here before you."

Soldier 2: "So you four have come here to borrow a ship to

sail over to the Western Continent, where you will then sneak into Stephis, and attempt an emergency rescue mission of Princess Mary? Just the four of you?"

Cid: "That is correct."

Soldier 1: "And both Lancelot and the queen agreed to this? What about backup? How many soldiers will join you on this mission?"

Thomas: "There are no other soldiers. Lindsea is in a crippled state right now. They need all possible soldiers to remain there in order to rebuild their defenses, and prepare for further attacks. Stephis can return at any time, and they need to be ready."

Soldier 2: "This is madness. It's a suicide mission. The four of you against all of Stephis. Surely you have seen what just happened to Lindsea."

Thomas: "I know you don't know us, but we have to do this. We knew the risks when we signed up for this job. Mary is in great danger, and we may be the only ones who can save her. We refuse to leave Stephis without her. No matter what it takes, we are going to get her out of there. She would do the same thing if it were any of us in her place."

Soldier 1: (Hands Thomas the letter.) "I have to say that I am truly amazed at your loyalty to the princess. You either have to be the bravest man alive, or a fool. How is it that we may help you?"

Thomas: "We came for a ship, and a crew to run it."

Soldier 1: "I can give you a ship, and two soldiers to navigate. Our ships are more advanced that the ones civilians might normally find at a ferry. Our soldiers are all trained to operate them, but you do need at least two men to do so."

Thomas: "That sounds great. Thank you."

Soldier 2: "Come. Let us show you to your ride, and introduce you to the crew. I wish there was more we could do for you."

Cid: "What you are doing is helpful. We will take what we can get."

Soldier 1: "Follow us please."

Scene 2: The Ocean

(Setting: In the middle of the ocean, between the Western and Eastern Continents. The party is sailing towards the Western Continent on their new boat. The two Lindsea soldiers are navigating and working the controls, while the party tries to plan their attack strategy for Stephis on deck. It is a bright and sunny day, with no clouds in the sky. A gentle breeze blows through the air, and the blue ocean waves are calm. The scene begins with the group sitting on deck, and talking.)

Dustin: "If we had brought the chocobos, we could get around faster."

Amanda: "But there would be five of them, along with four

of us, and they wouldn't be easy to hide."

Cid: "Yeah. Not to mention we would have to fit them on the boat here as well. We might move slower on foot, but we wouldn't be able to stay hidden. That won't go well at all."

Amanda: "We will have to sneak in, and sneak out. Quickly and quietly. I'm going to turn you all into thieves. Just like me."

Dustin: "Can you even make me into a thief?"

Amanda: "It's going to be my greatest challenge yet, but I do believe I can do it."

Dustin: "Wow. I've never been a thief before. Always figured I was too big for that."

Amanda: "That's why I said it will be a challenge."

Thomas: "I think we are starting to get off track here, folks. We left the chocobos at the stables in Lindsea so they can be taken care of while we are gone. They are definitely too much to be bringing along, and I would rather not put them at risk here either. Amanda is right. I think the best way to do this is to get in, and get out without being noticed. Or at least not noticed too much. If the whole army becomes aware of what we are doing, we might not make it out this time. I do expect that Mary will probably be heavily guarded though, wherever she is."

Cid: "We can't risk running into Nichols again either. Not with that spell he was using. Flare, I think it was."

Amanda: "That's right. I would almost give my right arm to learn that one. Almost. Maybe a few fingers."

Cid: "If he ever hits you with it you might just lose your fingers, and your arm."

(Everyone stops talking when they notice the ship in the distance. It looks huge, and it seems to be coming their way. Fast.)

Amanda: "That's a fancy ship over there. I haven't seen one like that before."

Cid: "It almost looks like it's coming straight at us."

Thomas: "I don't think they're from Stephis. And they probably aren't from Lindsea either."

Dustin: "Let's see what they do next."

(The party watches as the ship sails straight for them. As it gets closer, they notice the fancy wooden beams that make up the construction, along with the tall, elegant sails. The entire ship is painted black. The crow's nest sits high in the sky, and the tips of the cannons stick out both sides of the ship. The party watches in awe.)

Thomas: "I've never seen anything like it."

(They continue to stare as a black flag is hoisted up to the top of the sails. A white skull, with two crossing swords beneath it, are printed on both sides of the flag.)

Amanda: "Pirates!"

(The pirate ship makes a sudden turn, and starts firing its cannons toward the party. The cannon balls hit the boat, creating huge holes all over.)

Cid: "They're firing on us! What are we going to do?"

Amanda: "I don't know! We can't fight them from here!"

Thomas: "We're going to sink! Abandon ship!"

(The party members all jump off the sides of the boat, and land in the water. They try to swim away from it so they won't get hit with any cannon balls. They watch as the pirate ship stops firing, and sails right up against the boat. Grappling hooks fly through the air, and attach themselves to the boat. Several pirates swing over from their ship, and land on the boat.)

Dustin: "What are they doing?"

Thomas: "I think they just took over our boat!"

Dustin: "What are we doing?"

Thomas: "We're going to climb aboard, and take their ship!"

Cid: "You sure about that?"

Thomas: "We're going to try!"

Scene 3: The Nautilus

(Setting: On board the pirate ship, The Nautilus. The massive ship is completely built of black wooden beams. The black sails are flapping in the wind, along with the black pirate flag up above. The flag has a white skull on both sides, along with two crossing swords beneath it. The ship is quite large, and has nine cannons poking out of both sides. There is a pirate up in the crow's nest, and the rest are scrambling around on board. One can be seen at the helm, while the others are working in various locations on deck. There are several grappling hooks attached to the smaller ship from Lindsea, which is right alongside in the ocean. There are pirates on the deck of that ship as well, and several ropes dangling in the air from the swing over to the smaller ship. The four soaked party members are currently climbing up a rope ladder that is hanging over the railing, near the bow of the ship. The pirates are too occupied to notice them at the moment, so they are able to quietly climb aboard, and take out their weapons. It is bright and sunny out, and the wind is blowing strong as the scene begins.)

Dustin: "What's the plan?"

Thomas: "We need to take this ship somehow. But we can't kill them all."

Amanda: "Why not?"

Thomas: "It's too big, and I don't think the four of us alone can operate it."

Cid: "I'm not even sure if I can operate it."

(Everyone looks at Cid.)

Dustin: "This could be a problem. How are we going to convince all these pirates to sail the ship for us?"

Cid: "They did just put a bunch of holes in ours. I don't think they will be very cooperative. What if we just hide out on board, and sneak off the first chance we get?"

Amanda: "That sounds so boring! And what if they are heading the wrong way?"

Dustin: "That's very likely."

Thomas: "I say we cut down their numbers, and take their

captain prisoner."

Amanda: "Aaaarrrr! Now that's more like it! We'll make em walk the plank!"

Pirate 1: (Sneaks up behind Amanda.) "The only ones that be walking the plank this day will be you four scalawags!"

Amanda: (Spins around.) "Huh?"

Pirate 1: "Get em, boys!"

(A group of five pirates face off against the party. They are all armed with cutlasses, and are ready for blood.)

Amanda: "Careful with the... you know what. Pirates have a thing for treasure."

Thomas: "You mean the..."

Amanda: "Yeah. No magic. We can't afford to lose this ship either."

Dustin: "My axe is plenty sufficient for this job!"

Cid: "Just keep the hits off the beams! Wouldn't want to see this ship go down too."

(The party takes turns trading blows with their weapons against the pirates, who attack with their swords. They are careful not to reveal their Krystals, and refrain from using magic. Instead they turn to items, using potions for healing as needed. The pirates fight well, but are no match for the party. Cid's arrows are particularly effective from afar.

When the first group falls, another group of four pirates appear in their place.)

Cid: "They certainly have the numbers, even if they aren't that good."

Thomas: "What do you think, Cid? You'll be driving this ship."

Cid: "We should push toward the helm. Then maybe I can take control of the wheel."

(The party fights through the new group of pirates, using the same techniques. By now the others are becoming aware of their presence, and are making their way over. Once this group is down, the party is able to move a little closer toward the middle of the ship. Their progress is halted as another four pirates block their path.)

Amanda: "How many should we leave alive?"

Thomas: "I'm not even sure how many there are! Let's just keep moving forward!"

(The party quickly takes out the current group, then moves forward to meet with a new group of three. Two more come up from behind, and box them in.)

Amanda: "Now what?"

Thomas: "Two of us take the front, while the other two take the rear!"

(Thomas and Dustin attack the front group, who fight back

with their cutlasses. They take more damage now because of the higher numbers, but are able to take one pirate down. Amanda and Cid take one down in the rear.)

Cid: (Watches as another pirate joins with the rear group.) "This isn't going so well. Maybe we should use magic."

Thomas: "We are almost there! Just have to push through this bunch!"

(The party continues to fight off the pirates. They take down a few more on both sides. Thomas stops when he notices a new pirate appear up ahead.)

Thomas: "Check out that guy! He must be the captain!"

(Everyone looks toward the helm, and sees a pirate dressed in black. He is standing there with a serious look on his face, and is holding a fancy cutlass. He looks to his left, and raises his other arm. He slams his fist downward, then turns to look at the party once more. He watches as a huge black net comes falling down from above. It lands on the party, and snares all four of them in the ropes.)

Dustin: "What the?"

Amanda: "Don't worry! I'll get us out of here!"

(The four struggle to remove the ropes, but the net is large, and heavy. The more they move, the more tangled up they get. The pirates quickly surround them, and are grinning from ear to ear.)

Cid: "I think we just might have a problem here."

Scene 4: The Nautilus

(Setting: In the lower levels of the Nautilus. There is a small caged off section in the hold, right next to the ship's supplies. The black iron bars only have one locked door, and are situated in the back corner of the ship. It is slightly cold, and dark down here. There are a few flickering lanterns hanging from the wood beams above, providing the only light to this area. Crates and barrels full of supplies are stacked everywhere on this level. The lanterns are swaying side to side as the ship moves through the water, but everything else stays in place. The four party members are inside the cage. Amanda is lying down on a small straw bed, while the others are either sitting or standing. They have been down here for a while now, and haven't seen another person since the pirates locked them up. Scene begins with the group talking.)

Amanda: "Not gonna lie. I never saw this coming."

Dustin: "I really thought we had them."

Cid: (Sighs.) "How can we save Mary now? We are no better off than she is."

Amanda: (Thinking aloud.) "Parsley?"

Thomas: (Looks at Amanda, then at the others.) "Come on, guys. We've been through worse. We'll get out of this somehow. I know we will."

Amanda: "Parsnips..."

Dustin: "I can always just bust this door down!"

Thomas: "We still need this ship though. We can't risk doing anything that might make it sink."

Dustin: "Darn!"

Cid: "I'm glad we didn't bring the chocobos. That wouldn't have ended well."

Thomas: "I'll agree with that. At least we know they are safe."

Amanda: "Park? Party? Parlor?"

Cid: "What are you rambling about over there?"

Amanda: "Parlay! That's it! Parlay!"

Thomas: "Parlay?"

Amanda: "Yes. Parlay."

Dustin: "I still don't get it. Is this some sort of game?"

Amanda: (Sits up.) "No! Don't you guys know anything about pirates?"

Dustin: "Never seen them before."

Amanda: "It's part of the code! The pirate code!"

Cid: "Nope. Never heard of it."

Amanda: (Sighs.) "The pirate code is like the law for pirates. It tells them what they can and can't do. They aren't complete savages you know."

Thomas: (Listening.) "Go on."

Amanda: "Many years ago a man from my village was captured at sea by pirates. He eventually escaped, and came back to tell his tale."

Dustin: "What happened?"

Amanda: "He told us that if you ever find yourself captured by pirates, that you have to say the word, parlay."

Thomas: "What does that mean?"

Amanda: "It's part of the code. It means that you are exercising your right to speak to the captain without being harmed. It's your best chance to negotiate for your freedom. Before they do whatever they like to you."

Cid: "I've never heard you speak like this before. You sound so educated."

Amanda: (Sticks her tongue out at Cid.)

Cid: "That's better."

Thomas: "So all we have to do is say the word, and we can speak to the captain?"

Amanda: "It's that simple. But only one of us can go."

(Everyone looks at each other.)

Dustin: "I vote for Thomas."

Thomas: "What?"

Cid: "I second that."

Amanda: "And me!"

Thomas: "Now wait a minute here."

Amanda: "If anyone has a chance of getting us out of here, it's you."

Cid: "She speaks the truth."

Dustin: "Definitely."

Thomas: "Oh man."

(Everyone stops talking when they hear a hatch open in the distance, and footsteps coming down the stairs. They all look at Thomas. A lone pirate is holding up a lantern as he makes his way toward the cell.)

Dustin: "You're up, T!"

Scene 5: The Nautilus

(Setting: Inside the officer's quarters in the rear of the ship. The pirate captain, Black Bart, is standing next to an oval table, examining a map of the Western Continent. He is dressed in black clothing, and wears a black handled cutlass on his belt. His long black mustache curls up at both ends. The first mate is standing there with him. They are discussing their plans to invade Stephis, so that they can recover their stolen treasure. The quarters mostly consists of ornately carved wooden furniture. The table, a desk, two chairs, and a few bookcases are arranged around the room. The table is in the center, and the desk is off to the right of the double doors. There is a small chest next to the desk, which is empty of gil. A wooden barrel full of rolled up paper maps sits between two bookcases on the opposite side of the room. On top of the table sits a compass, while a dagger, jammed into the map, marks the location of Stephis Castle. Burning lanterns sway side to side as they hang down from above. The scene begins with the two men talking.)

Bart: (Pointing to the map.) "If we come down from the north, we can follow the river, and come out to the west of the castle. The trees should hide us well enough to get close to them without being seen."

First Mate: "Aye. It does seem the best path."

(The two men stop, and look up as another pirate enters through the double doors. He walks right up to the table, and begins to speak.)

Pirate: "Captain! The new prisoners are claiming their right to parlay."

Bart: "Are they now? That is interesting."

Pirate: "What are your orders?"

Bart: "Bring their leader to me. Leave the others in the hold."

Pirate: "Aye, sir!" (Exits through the doors.)

First Mate: "Do you really think this wise, captain? Meeting with Lindsea soldiers at a time like this?"

Bart: "These are no ordinary soldiers. They don't look like them. They don't act like them. I think there is something else going on here, and this could be my only chance to find out what. Besides, only pirates know about the code."

First Mate: "Been a long time since anyone spoke the word, parlay."

Bart: "Aye. No real soldier from Stephis or Lindsea would ever think to use such words. If this crew isn't part of either kingdom, then who are they with? And why were they sailing on a ship from Lindsea? There's only one way to find out."

~~~~~~~~~~

A little while later...

(Thomas enters through the double doors of the officer's quarters. A pirate is walking behind him with his sword out. Black Bart is sitting in a chair behind the desk, and motions for Thomas to come over to sit across from him. The other pirate follows closely behind.)

Bart: "Leave us."

Pirate: "Aye." (He puts his sword back in his scabbard, and exits the room.)

Bart: "So what could a small group of warriors, traveling aboard a ship from Lindsea, but not being Lindsea soldiers themselves, who are familiar in the ways of pirates, possibly be up to?"

Thomas: "I could ask you the same thing, captain. Why would a lone pirate ship be sailing these waters at such a time as these, when the kingdoms of Stephis and Lindsea are at war with each other? A ship who so blatantly attacks the very kingdom that is trying to restore peace and order to the world?"

Bart: "Is that so? I see no peace and order here. The two great kingdoms have been fighting for power and control ever since the beginning of time. They don't care about us. They don't care about freedom. All they want is to rule the world. My job is to make sure that people see that true freedom is right here. On this ship. In these waters. Not in serving some king or queen that couldn't care less about them."

Thomas: "So you don't belong to either kingdom? You don't fight for either one?"

Bart: "Never! I serve only freedom. To go where you want, to do what you please, to find true happiness in this world."

Thomas: "But there won't be any freedom if things continue as they are. The direction that Stephis is headed, the plans that Nichols and Edward have for the world. If they win, then it's all over. We either end up as slaves, or dead. Or worse, as monsters fighting for them."

Bart: "Who are you? And what are you doing out here on my ship, speaking to me in strange words?"

Thomas: "My name is Thomas, and we were headed to Stephis to rescue a friend of ours that is being held prisoner there. That is until you attacked our ship."

Bart: "They call me Black Bart. I am the captain of this ship, the Nautilus. I have spent the last part of my life as a prisoner of Lindsea, and I have only just recently been set free. I too am headed for Stephis."

Thomas: "You won't be able to reach it on this ship. You will have to travel over land. I know. I was once a prisoner there, but I also escaped."

Bart: "It seems we have more than a few things in common. Stephis is currently holding on to certain possessions of mine, and I come to take them back. The treasure, mind you."

Thomas: "You will have to make it past the entire Stephis army, the town, and the castle. Do you have any idea what you are getting yourself into? I was there at the battle of Lindsea. I saw what they can do."

Bart: "Likewise for you. How do you intend to rescue your friend with just four warriors? It can't be done."

Thomas: "An intelligent man would look at this situation, and decide that the best way to do this would be for both of us to join forces. Separately, we might fail. But together, there is hope."

Bart: "That is quite an offer you have there. What is it you propose?"

Thomas: "That you set my friends and I free, and together we sail for Stephis, and invade the castle. We save our friend, and you take back your treasure."

Bart: "How do I know that I can trust you to keep your

word?"

Thomas: "How do I know that I can trust you?"

Bart: (Opens up a desk drawer, and takes out an old book. He lays it on the desk, and slides it over to Thomas.) "If you are as good a fighter as I think you are, then tell me what this is."

Thomas: (Takes the book, and looks it over.) "This is a spell book. It allows the user to cast stop magic. This has to be a time spell."

Bart: "Can you do anything with it?"

Thomas: "I can. All of us are able to learn, and use magic. Can you?"

Bart: "Not me. There is no magic aboard this ship. We fight with our blades. But I will give you this book as a sign of trust, in the hopes that you will use it in our fight against Stephis."

Thomas: "And I can give you something in return as well. My friend that we are going to rescue is the princess of Lindsea. You said you were once a prisoner there."

Bart: "Aye. It was a matter of luck that I escaped during the battle. But I have no doubt they would put me away again if they ever get the chance."

Thomas: "If you help us save Mary, I promise on my life that you will be pardoned of all crimes against Lindsea, and will no longer have to fear being captured again."

Bart: "I fear nothing in this world. However, that is quite the statement you made there. Do you even have the power to make such promises?"

Thomas: "I don't, but Mary does. We just helped prevent the destruction of Lindsea. We are on our way now to save their princess. Maybe you don't know her, and maybe you don't trust her, but I do. She is not like the others. She will help you. I give you my word, or my life."

Bart: "Then I accept your offer. I will send word to my men to release your friends. We will set sail for Stephis immediately."

Thomas: "Do you have a plan of attack yet?"

Bart: "We are working on that right now."

Thomas: "When the others are out, we should take a look at that map of yours. We've all escaped from Stephis twice now. We can do it again."

Bart: "Aye. Let's do."

Act 3:
SNEAKING IN

Scene 1: Stephis Castle

(Setting: The dungeon on the lower levels of Stephis Castle. The walls, the floor, and the ceiling are made of stone. Black iron cells are arranged on both sides of the hallways throughout. It is a cold and dark place down here. A few torches are lit up along the walls, but most are burned out. The air is filled with the moans and groans of the prisoners. Some have been down here for years, having been forgotten by the world. Prisoners are all over. Some are in the cells, and some are chained to the walls, either by their hands, their feet, or both. A number of people are Lindsea soldiers who were captured at some point during the battle of Lindsea. Puddles of water are all over, as there are several leaks in the walls. Each drop of water can be heard as it hits the floor. The people who are closest to them attempt to stretch out a hand to take a drink, although it isn't much. A damp and musty smell also floats through the air. Two Stephis soldiers suddenly enter the dungeon, and they are bringing a new prisoner along with them. A black hood covers the person's head, preventing any sight, or knowledge of the location. They walk the prisoner to an occupied cell, and unlock the door. After a gentle push inside, one of the soldiers removes the hood, while the other locks the door shut. The two soldiers exit the dungeon, right before the scene begins. The old female prisoner in the cage starts talking to her new cell mate once the coast is clear.)

Prisoner 1: (After examining the newcomer.) "Princess Mary? Is that you?"

Mary: (Tries to fix her hair so she can see again, now that the hood is off.) "Yes. I am Mary. Where am I?"

Prisoner 1: (Bows.) "Highness. This is the castle dungeon. What happened? Why are you here?"

Mary: "I was captured during the battle of Lindsea. Stephis soldiers brought me here, and have kept me prisoner ever since. They keep moving me around, and I never know where I am, or where I am going next."

Prisoner 1: "I am sorry, your majesty. They took me back in Lindsea town. I was injured, but they had mercy on me. Many of us came from the town. Now we sit here day to day, wondering if we will ever be saved."

Mary: "I must confess that I'm also worried about the situation. I know it isn't very princess like for me to say such things, but it's true. I miss my friends, and I miss my freedom."

Prisoner 1: (Wraps her arms around Mary as she starts to cry.) "There, there, dear. You might be royalty, but you are still human. And I am still old enough to be your grandmother. Everyone could use a caring hug from time to time."

Mary: (Wipes her tears away.) "Thank you. I'm afraid I don't even know your name."

Prisoner 1: "My name is Harriet, dear."

Mary: "Well, Harriet, it's nice to meet you. I know things seem rough right now, but I still have hope that we will get through this. No matter how bad things are, or how long we must suffer, I still believe that my friends will come."

Harriet: "You must have some really great friends to be that sure. Are they from the castle? Are they soldiers?"

Mary: "Kind of. They are from all over the world. But we have been through much together, and we have survived many dangerous battles. Together, we are unstoppable."

Harriet: "It sounds like they are an amazing bunch. I am glad to hear that there are still good people in the world. Especially now, when everything seems so dark."

Mary: "Yes. These truly are dark times."

Harriet: "Are you hungry, dear? I have a bit of bread stashed away if you like."

Mary: "Oh no! I couldn't possibly take your food. It must be hard to come by."

Harriet: "Please. I insist. You look famished."

(Harriet walks over to her straw bed, and pulls a cloth wrapped loaf of bread out from under the pillow. She carries it back to Mary, and unwraps it. Mary immediately gets a whiff of it.)

Mary: "That does smell amazing. I bet it tastes just as good too."

Harriet: (Hands Mary the loaf.) "Here. Take it."

Mary: "Are you sure? I just don't feel right about it."

Harriet: "Dear, you need your strength. Both now, and when your friends arrive to bust us out of here." (She winks.) "I'm counting on them as well now. You have me persuaded."

Mary: (Takes the bread, and starts eating.) "Thank you, Harriet. This does help."

Harriet: "That's what friends are for."

Scene 2: The Woods

(Setting: Inside the forest to the west of Stephis Castle. The party has set up camp along with Black Bart and his crew. They are all staying inside a group of tents until they are ready to continue. It is currently late at night, and the only light comes from the single lantern in each tent. The clouds above are hiding the moon and stars on this warm, and humid night. The scene begins inside Bart's tent, where the four party members are gathered around a small table with him. They are looking over a map of Stephis, and are discussing their next move. The rest of the crew are all asleep in their tents.)

Bart: "There are several issues here. First, we need to get inside the castle. After that, we need to find the treasure, and rescue your friend."

Thomas: "The last time we snuck inside it was from the town. Wait... that was in the future."

Bart: "Huh?"

Cid: "I never actually went in the castle, but Mary and I did find a suitable place in the bushes to eavesdrop outside the dining room window. That almost seems like ages ago."

Bart: "How easy would it be to get in through there?"

Cid: "Not easy at all. The windows have bars on them. I think they all do."

Amanda: "That's right. Windows won't work."

Thomas: "This is certainly difficult because there aren't that many of us, and we don't know where Mary is. Or the treasure."

Dustin: "There are several prisons around here too. She could be at any one of them."

Amanda: "Or at the monster factory if that's what they've decided to do with her. We might have to search the whole place."

Cid: "They might even be keeping her in the town. As for the treasure, who knows where that is."

Amanda: "I'm pretty sure they would keep that in the castle. I happen to know that they do have a treasury. And a dungeon on the lowest level. Kind of like Lindsea."

Bart: "Have you been inside either one?"

Amanda: "I never made it that far. Luckily."

Cid: "This is a big area to cover. It could be a problem trying to sneak through with so many of us here."

Bart: "I think we might do better to break up into smaller groups. Each group can search a different part of the town, and the castle. We can cover more area in less time."

Thomas: "What are you thinking?"

Bart: "We should all break up into groups of two, and search our designated areas. Once we find what we are looking for, we get back to the ship. Since we had to leave some of the crew behind to guard the ship, that leaves us with ten groups of two."

Dustin: "So we aren't here to crush the remaining Stephis army, and burn this place to the ground?"

Bart: "Definitely not. We don't have the numbers, or the equipment. Besides, my crew wouldn't dare attempt such things. They are only here for the treasure. Same as I."

Thomas: "I agree. We are only here for Mary. This isn't the time to take down Edward and Nichols. We can do that later."

Amanda: "Ok. So you are saying that each of us will grab a partner, and take our own area on the map to search for

Mary, and the treasure?"

Bart: "Aye."

Amanda: "Sweet. I claim Cid."

Cid: "Excuse me?"

Amanda: "You heard me."

Thomas: "I guess we just have to pick our locations then. And then decide who goes with who."

Amanda: "I want to go with Cid."

Cid: "Really?"

Dustin: "Do you think the other pirates will agree with this plan?"

Bart: "I'm the captain here. They will follow my orders. I just hope each of you is as capable of this mission as I think you are."

Amanda: "Aye, captain. I'm ready when you are."

Thomas: "Does everyone agree with this plan before we continue on? We all need to feel comfortable about it first since it will split us up a lot. We are already one short with Mary gone. The good thing is that it will be more challenging for Stephis to keep up with us while we are all spread out. It would force them to decrease their numbers too if they end up coming after us. But let's just hope we don't have to deal with them at all. Just get in, and get out."

Dustin: "I think I can handle it."

Cid: "Me too."

Amanda: "Let me at em!"

Thomas: "Ok. We should get some sleep now. It's getting late. We can continue our planning tomorrow."

Scene 3: Stephis Castle

(Setting: The next day, inside the scroll room on the second floor of Stephis Castle. There is a large oval table in the center of the room. The top currently has several rolled up scrolls on it, along with some open maps, and small stacks of books. There are several wooden chairs surrounding the table. The walls are lined with bookshelves, and most of them are filled with books, and rolled up scrolls. On the wall with the closed wooden door there are torches burning, and giving light to the room. There are four men standing around the table, looking over the maps. King Edward, Nichols, Daevas, and Alistair are here. They are discussing the current situation in Stephis, and making plans for the future of the kingdom. Edward is wearing his red robe, while Nichols has on the usual black hooded robe. Daevas is wearing a half suit of armor, while Alistair has all white clothing on. The scene begins with them talking.)

Edward: "It seems we may need some time to recover from the recent battle. We may have lost this one, but it will not be the last."

Daevas: "It wasn't a complete loss, sire. Our army remains at about seventy percent. We managed to do quite a bit of damage to the town, and the castle. It's going to take them a lot of time to rebuild. Although we lost some men and equipment, at least Stephis remains whole."

Edward: "You do have a point. We underestimated their numbers, and their resolve. Once we are able rebuild our army though, we will attack yet again."

Nichols: "I was so close to getting my hands on that white Krystal. It was right there in front of me. But that Thomas and friends... once again they have foiled my plans."

Alistair: "We might not have recovered the white Krystal, but capturing Princess Mary is almost as satisfying. Perhaps more."

Nichols: "How is that?"

Alistair: "Just think of the possibilities. We have so many options now. We can keep her prisoner, turn her into a monster to join our army, or perhaps make her into the next assassin to send out after Thomas. We know so much more now, and there is so much more we can do."

Daevas: "We could always just kill her, but I don't see any

benefit to that right now. We would be better off holding her for ransom, or perhaps we could use her to get the Krystal."

Edward: "How would we do that?"

Daevas: "We can make an offer to trade. We give Mary back in exchange for the Krystal. Assuming Lindsea still has it. If Thomas has it, we offer to deal with him."

Edward: "I'd just as soon kill her and be done with it, but I do see your point. She will definitely be worth something to somebody."

Alistair: "What about trading her in exchange for the complete and total surrender of Lindsea, with all properties included?"

Edward: "Now I see why Nichols picked you to be in charge of the monster factory. I like the way you think."

Alistair: "What can I say? Running the factory gives me lots of time to think these days."

Nichols: "It seems we will need a little longer to consider what to do with the princess then. In the mean time, I suggest we keep moving her around frequently. Very frequently. We can't afford to have Thomas break her out like the last time."

Edward: "That was unfortunate. We underestimated them back then. We cannot make the same mistake again."

Daevas: "Yes, majesty. My men have been charged with

irregularly regularly moving her between all prisons. Both day, and night. She has no way of knowing when or where she will be moved. And with the increase in prisoners at the moment, it will be even harder to find her."

Alistair: "I do hope that I might have some of those new prisoners to help rebuild the monster army. These things take time you know. More time than it takes to prepare a human soldier."

Edward: "Yes. There are plenty of choices available to you. As you find ones you like, you may have them. All the others will either end up as slaves, or they will just rot in their cells most likely."

Nichols: "HA HA HA!"

Alistair: "Pardon me, sire, but didn't we come here to discuss the maps?"

Nichols: "Yes! I almost forgot."

(The four men huddle around the map of Stephis town that is lying open on the table.)

Nichols: "Hmmm. There really is no room inside the town. It might work better to do this just outside. But where exactly?"

Daevas: "How big are we trying to build this thing?"

Edward: "The treasure room is quite full at the moment. I am willing to spend as much as is needed in order to do this right. We need to prepare for mass production, along with the addition of the white Krystal. Once we find it of course."

Nichols: "Of course."

Alistair: (Points to a section between the town, and the castle.) "There ought to be enough room right here. My perfect building would have five stories. But that would just draw too much attention to it. Perhaps we might start with less, and leave space to add on to later. Or we can work on building up the town as well. That way the new monster factory doesn't stick out as much."

Nichols: "The current building is still useful. We might just have to use both for the moment, until we can safely build up the new one later. I do agree that a single new building that is taller than the castle would draw too much attention. Especially from Thomas and his friends, should they ever decide to show up."

Daevas: "We also don't need another target for Lindsea either, should they ever decide to attack."

Edward: "I don't believe they would dare attempt such a thing right now, but anything is possible these days."

Nichols: "If everyone is in agreement then, I will begin to scout out the area shortly."

Edward: "I will take a look at the treasury, and hire the builders."

Alistair: "I guess I'll start checking out the prisons for some possible new monsters."

Daevas: "And I will check on the current location of Mary, and make sure she is moved again. She will be switched around daily if needed."

Edward: (Claps his hands.) "Gentlemen, it sounds like a plan. Let us get to work."

Scene 4: Stephis Town

(Setting: Inside a small prison in the town. It is day time, and the sun is shining in through the barred windows. This prison is tiny compared to the castle dungeon, and it only holds two cells on one side. On the other side there is an old man chained to the wall, and he is currently sitting on the floor. There is a small table and chair in the middle of the room. The side with the single wooden door has the two barred windows, and the opposite side is plain. The front door opens up, and in walks Mary with a black hood on again. The two Stephis soldiers behind her lead her to the first cell. One soldier opens the door, while the other removes the hood. They untie her hands, and direct her into the cell. After locking the door, they start back for the front door.)

Soldier 1: "I wonder when we'll have to move her again. Seems like we just moved her."

Soldier 2: "We did just move her."

(Mary watches from her cell as the two soldiers exit the prison. When the door locks from the outside, she looks around the building. It doesn't look familiar. She also notices the old man sitting on the floor opposite her. His old brown garments are dirty and torn. His hair and his beard are long, and scraggly. His head is down, and he is looking at the ground.)

Mary: "Stephis has so many prisons. This must be like the fifth one I've been in so far."

(The old man slowly raises his head, and looks around the room. Mary stays quiet while she observes him. He looks right at her, but it's almost as if he can't see her there. He seems to be staring off into space. She wonders if something is wrong with him.)

Old Man: "My... I haven't heard that voice in so many years."

Mary: "Do I know you from somewhere?"

Old Man: "You used to know me. The old me. Before they beat me, and broke me, and left me here to die."

(Mary tries to think about who he could possibly be. She studies him, and though he isn't what she remembers, she thinks she has figured it out.)

Mary: "Doctor Tot? Is that you?"

Tot: "I've missed you, princess. This world is no longer the place we once knew. And knowing where you are right now, only discourages me more. Nevertheless, it is so good to hear your voice again."

Mary: "I can't believe I've found you! Since you left the castle those years ago, I have often wondered about you. I never knew where you went, or if you would ever come back again."

Tot: "Tell me... are we alone in here?"

Mary: "Yes. Why?"

Tot: "You must forgive me. They have taken my sight, so I can no longer see."

Mary: "Oh, that's horrible!"

Tot: "We have no time to waste. If you are still the same Mary that I know and love, then I have much to tell you. I may never make it out of here, but for you I still have hope. You used to tell me many things when you were young. You had revealed your heart to me quite often. I need to know one thing. Do you still wish to save the world?"

Mary: "With everything that I am."

Tot: "Then you must know where I have been. At the time I left you, I sensed that a great evil was upon us. I knew that Lindsea would be in great danger if I didn't act. Not only the kingdom, but also the world. So I packed up my things, and went on a quest."

Mary: "A quest for what?"

Tot: "A weapon. One that is so powerful, it would ensure the safety of the kingdom forever."

Mary: "A weapon? Like a sword?"

Tot: "Not a sword. A crystal."

Mary: "My friends and I, we have been searching for the Krystals too. The Master Krystals. Like the ones you told me about. They really exist! We already found three of them, and we are sure that Stephis has the fourth."

Tot: "Are they safe?"

Mary: "Yes. We have them hidden away."

Tot: "Good. You must be very careful with them, princess. You must be careful who you trust as well. The Krystals are mighty powerful, and they are known to corrupt even the strongest of men."

Mary: "I will. Have you found one? We are still missing the blue, and the black one."

Tot: "I am afraid I have not. I was never searching for the Master Krystals. I was only trying to find a summoning crystal. The garnet scepter that holds the spirit of Bahamut. The great dragon."

Mary: "Bahamut? Did you find it?"

Tot: "No, I did not. I was found out, and imprisoned before I had the chance. But not before I managed to find this."

(Mary watches as Tot reaches inside his garment, and pulls out a small bracer. It is covered in tiny diamonds, and sparkles in the sunlight. Mary can feel her chest getting warmer, and looks down to see what's happening. Her moonstone pendant has a light yellow glow to it, and is warm to the touch.)

Mary: "What is that? And why is my pendant glowing all of a sudden?"

Tot: "Alexander must feel the presence of another Eidolon. It is a relief to know you haven't lost him. This bracer that I have, and the diamonds that cover it, hold the spirit of Ramuh. The Eidolon of thunder and lightning."

Mary: "What are you going to do with it?"

Tot: "I can't do anything with it. I've just been keeping it safe until I find someone who can. I would like to give it to you, but I am afraid I can't reach you."

Mary: "I know. I'm sorry. If there were any way to get it from you, and get us out of here I would. But I am afraid they will come back to move me again soon."

Tot: "I do know where Bahamut rests though. I may not have found the scepter, but I do know where it is. It is buried in a desert to the north of here. There is an island, one that is very difficult to reach, and one that is perhaps the most dangerous place on the planet. You can be assured that everything on the island will be after you to kill you. Plants and animals alike. It's the land of the giants."

Mary: "Giants?"

Tot: "I am afraid so. If you wish to continue my quest, that is where you must go. As for me, I am afraid it is too late to be of much use."

Mary: "Doctor Tot... I wish you had told me back then. I could have helped you. Things could have been different now."

Tot: "Maybe so, Mary. But I had to protect you. Protect the kingdom. I cannot bear the thought of Lindsea falling. It is my home. Though one that I will never see again."

Mary: (With tears in her eyes.) "My friends will come, Doctor Tot. They will save us. I believe it with my whole heart. We will return to Lindsea once again. I promise you."

Tot: "I trust you, Mary. I will wait patiently, and hope that they arrive quickly. While there is still time."

Scene 5: Stephis Town

(Setting: It is early evening in Stephis town. The sun has just disappeared in the distance, and the darkness is covering the land. It is cloudy outside, and the moon and stars are hidden. The town itself is about medium size. Not nearly as big as Lindsea, but much bigger than the others on the Western Continent. Stephis is a battle centered kingdom, and it shows. The town is a mix of houses and stores, but most of the buildings are for training, and weapon storage. There are multiple barracks, archery ranges, stables, and siege workshops. There are a few weapon stores, magic shops, and item shops. There are also numerous prisons, along with the discreetly hidden monster factory. Most of the buildings are made of bricks, but the houses are made of sticks and stones. The whole town is made up of brick roads and pathways. There are some farms and mills on the outside of town, along with some mining camps closer to the mountains. A lumber mill is near the woods as well. The castle can be seen to the north of town. There are burning torches along the roads, and near the doors of the buildings. The scene begins with Amanda and Cid creeping through the shadows.)

Amanda: (Freezes in place alongside a brick building.) "Hold it, you dirty dog."

(Amanda and Cid lean up against the wall, hiding themselves in the darkness. They both wait there until two soldiers pass by.)

Amanda: "Avast! Continue on!"

(Cid follows Amanda through the town. He isn't too impressed with her attempts to act like a pirate, but he is willing to deal with it so they can complete their mission.)

Amanda: "We'll search the whole town. Any prisons we find could be holding Mary. And any treasure chests we come across, we empty them. Savvy?"

Cid: "Aye. How do you think the others are doing?"

Amanda: "Probably about the same. I wouldn't mind taking down some of these soldiers, but I guess we should stick to the plan."

Cid: "Yeah. Just need to find some disguises first. I wonder if it would work better to dress as soldiers, or townsfolk."

Amanda: "Soldiers. Then we can go anywhere we want."

Cid: "We just have to be sure we aren't attacking our own guys. Let's follow those two over there, and take them down."

(Amanda and Cid stay in the shadows, and follow two soldiers that are passing by a weapon store. One of them stops in front of the Inn, while the other continues down the road. Cid takes out his bow and arrows, and shoots one toward the distracted fellow. Amanda quickly runs up behind him, and slices him up with her daggers. When he falls, Cid comes over to join her.)

Cid: "Same plan on the other one."

(Cid prepares another arrow, and fires toward the soldier in the distance. Amanda runs up to him, and delivers the sneak attack from behind. When the guy is down, Amanda looks back at Cid. Both of them grab their downed soldiers, and drag them into the shadows.)

Amanda: (While pulling off the man's armor.) "Yuck. Sweaty soldier armor."

(Cid and Amanda each remove all the armor, and put the pieces on themselves. Then they head toward each other, and meet in the middle.)

Amanda: "It's kind of big for me."

Cid: "Me too. And heavy."

Amanda: "Don't be such a wuss. We've got work to do."

Cid: "Yes. Mary, here we come!"

~~~~~~~~~~

Meanwhile... in another part of town...

Dustin: "I can't wait to bust some Stephis skulls!"

Thomas: "Easy there, big fella. It's too early for that. Maybe if things go south near the end we can do some damage, but for now we need to keep it down."

Dustin: "Yeah. Hey, you remember when we all first met? We were trying to rescue Mary then too!"

Thomas: "I guess the more things change, the more they stay the same."

Dustin: "I'm not so sure about this disguise idea. I don't think I can find an outfit big enough for me here."

Thomas: "We'll just have to do our best. If we go for the soldiers, you can probably work with some armor. Might not be a full suit, but we'll see."

(Thomas leads the way through the buildings. Dustin has a harder time staying hidden, but there aren't too many people out at this time. The fiery torches that are all over are giving off a lot of light. They both try their best to avoid them, along with the people.)

Dustin: "Hey, Thomas. Do you really think we can find her? It's not quite like the last time."

Thomas: "You're right. It isn't. All I know is that we have to find her. I want her back with us. I miss her smile. And her excitement. She's always so positive, and she cares about everyone."

Dustin: "She always has so much hope too. And she motivates us to keep fighting. Even when it's hard."

(Thomas and Dustin pause behind a building while some townsfolk walk by. Thomas is glad it's dark out, because that way Dustin can't see the tears filling up his eyes. He tries to wipe them clean before they continue on.)

Thomas: "If Nichols manages to turn Mary into another Lilith to go after us... I will never forgive him. And I will never stop until he is found, and destroyed."

Dustin: "I know. And I will be right there with you. We all will."

Thomas: (Stops.) "Look! Two soldiers over there. Let's take them down."

Dustin: "With pleasure."

~~~~~~~~~~

And in another part of town...

Bart: "There it is, men! The castle!"

(Bart and his pirate crew take a look at the castle in the distance, from their hiding places on the farm. None of them have ever been inside Stephis Castle before. Some have been in the town at one point in their lives, but the castle is all new.)

Pirate 1: "It looks mighty big from here, captain."

Bart: "Indeed it is. We'll stick to the plan. Six of you will take to the town, and the rest of you will follow me to the castle. I want you all in teams of two, and be sure to keep your distance. We need to cover the whole place before morning, and make it back to camp before the sun rises."

Pirates: "Aye."

Bart: "I don't expect us to recover all of our lost treasure exactly, but we will recover some treasure no doubt. I want you to take everything you find in a treasure chest, or in the treasury. Everything you can carry, take it with you. Anything made of gold or jewels, and of course gil. Take what you can!"

Pirates: "Give nothing back!"

Bart: "And be on the lookout for a princess appearing woman. She goes by the name of Mary. If you should find her locked away somewhere, be sure and report it back to me. The others are in need of saving her. Any questions?"

Pirates: "No, captain!"

Bart: "Then... let us commence."

Act 4: THE RESCUE

Scene 1: The Desert

(Setting: The great desert island to the north of the Eastern Continent. There is a huge slave camp set up in the sands. It is night time, and fiery torches are burning bright throughout the scene. The light wind is causing the fire to dance all around. There are tents set up all over, with makeshift wooden structures and equipment nearby. A number of people are asleep in the tents, but several are still up, and hard at work. There are two groups of human slaves here. The night workers, and the day workers. The night workers are scattered all around, and are currently digging in several locations. Piles of sand and broken up rocks are everywhere. The slaves are dressed in dirty rags, while the giant overseers are armed with enormous whips. The ends of their whips are equipped with various sharp objects such as rocks, shells, and bones. One of the giants is dressed differently than the others, but Hrungnir isn't just any giant. He is the king of their kind. He is wearing brown shorts, and boots almost up to his knees. His forearms are covered with brown leather bracers, and he's wearing a helmet with a horn coming out of both sides. His bare chest is covered in hair. He is not here to oversee the slaves, but to check on the whole operation, which was his own design. Hrungnir carries an enormous spear, which is even taller than he is. As he walks through the sand, the slaves cower under his great size, and presence. The scene begins as Hrungnir approaches one of the overseers.)

Overseer 1: (Bows.) "Master."

Hrungnir: "What progress have you made in this sector?"

Overseer 1: "The slaves are working at all hours of the day, and night, master."

Hrungnir: "And? Have you found anything?"

Overseer 1: "Not yet. We are getting close though. The farther down the men dig, the more signs of life they are discovering."

Hrungnir: "What sort of signs?"

Overseer 1: "You know, evidence that people once lived here. Tools, pottery, weapons. Skeletons."

Hrungnir: "No signs of the hidden fortress though?"

Overseer 1: "Not here. Not yet."

Hrungnir: "We must find the ruins first, and only then will I be able to recover the scepter."

Overseer 1: "How sure are you that these ruins actually still exist? And this scepter you speak of?"

Hrungnir: "It is here. This I know. We just have to find it is all. That's why I have set up dig sites in all the most likely locations on the island. We start with these first, and if we are unsuccessful, we will try new locations next."

(The two giants turn to see another overseer headed their way.)

Overseer 2: (Bows.) "Master."

Hrungnir: "What news do you bring?"

Overseer 2: "I just wanted to say that I believe our progress could be greater if it weren't for these same two problems that we've been having. The first would be these human slaves. They are just so whiny and weak. And the more we beat them, the slower they seem to work."

Hrungnir: "You might just need to come up with a little extra motivation for them. Perhaps you could threaten to take their lives, or the lives of their loved ones. That tends to work. Especially when you set some examples right in front of them."

Overseer 1: "He he he."

Overseer 2: "The other issue I've noticed, as you probably

also have, are the other monsters on this island. Many of them keep attacking the camp, and the slaves. Some of the larger ones like the sand worms have really been affecting our progress. They keep moving the sand around after we have cleared it, and then they keep breaking our equipment. That's when they aren't trying to eat the slaves."

Hrungnir: "That is a problem. Slaves are hard to come by, and it takes a lot of work to get more equipment out here. Let me think about that, and see if I can come up with some ideas. They don't call this the Forbidden Continent for nothing."

Overseer 1: "He does have a point about the monsters. And speaking of points, those pesky little cactuars keep getting their needles all over the place. I just hope one of the jumbo ones don't show up near here. The camp might not survive that kind of an attack."

(The conversation stops when several screams are heard in the distance. All the slaves stop working, and peer off into the darkness to find the source of them. A number of slaves suddenly start running toward this end of the camp from the other side. Some of the overseers here step out in front to block their path. That causes them to slide to a halt. Everyone turns to look at them, and notices the great fear on their faces.)

Hrungnir: (Steps toward the slaves.) "What is the meaning of this commotion?"

Slave 1: (Bows.) "My lord, there is a most hideous creature who appeared in the darkness. I know that normally they don't come so close to the camp at night, but we must have gotten too close to something. This beast, it blew some sort of gas upon us, and the men just went crazy! They all started attacking each other! A few of us managed to escape."

Slave 2: (Bows.) "It is true, my lord. This beast is preventing us from moving any farther. The others are already dead!"

Hrungnir: (Points to the two overseers he has been talking to.) "You two! Come with me! We will remove this beast so that our work may continue."

Overseer 1: (Gulp.) "Yes, sire."

(A small crowd follows from behind as Hrungnir leads the way to the other side of the camp. The slaves who escaped from the beast also come along to point the way. When they approach the scene, the fallen slaves start to become visible to everyone.)

Hrungnir: (Wields his giant spear.) "Who dares to disturb my operation, and slay my workers?"

Unknown Creature: (Speaking from the darkness.) "You do not belong here. None of you do. This is our island. You need to leave. Or else."

Hrungnir: "You dare to threaten me? You don't know who you are talking to, nor do you understand the power which I command. Come on out, and face me!"

(Everyone watches as a huge plant like monster emerges into the torch light. It has several tentacles for legs, and its head is like that of a sea anemone, with a very large mouth. The enormous mouth is full of razor sharp teeth, and the tongue sticks out as it speaks.)

Unknown Creature: "This island, and the secrets that are buried here, are not to be taken lightly. I may be the first malboro you have seen, but I can promise you that I will not be the last."

Hrungnir: "This day will be your last!"

(Hrungnir and the two overseers begin to transform out of their human forms. Their already large heights start to increase. They all become both wider, and taller. Their heads and necks grow longer, and their mouths fill with sharp teeth. A tail appears behind each of them, along with fur all over. Their fingernails turn to claws. The human slaves back away from them all as they witness the transformation. The three beasts start to attack the malboro. Hrungnir has his spear, and the other two their whips.)

Malboro: "What are you? I've never seen your kind before."

Hrungnir: "We are behemoths. The last of our kind. And I am the king. Prepare to meet your doom!"

(Hrungnir lunges at the malboro with his spear. The beast hits with such power that the plant is knocked back.)

Malboro: "See how you like the taste of my Bad Breath!"

(The giant plant opens up his mouth, and a black mist comes pouring out over the behemoths. The three are immediately hit with a mixture of negative status effects. Poison, darkness, and silence affect them all. Hrungnir takes out a remedy, and uses it on himself. After a flash of white light, all of his status effects quickly disappear.)

Hrungnir: "Your tricks won't work on us! Prepare to die!"

(One of the overseers attacks with his whip, but misses due to his blindness. The other one manages to hit the malboro despite his blindness. Hrungnir takes his spear, and delivers the final blow. They all watch as the plant creature falls, sending up a cloud of dust into the air.)

Malboro: "Such strength..."

(Everyone watches as the creature dies. The slaves are petrified of the behemoths now, even more so than the malboro. The three beasts return to their normal human forms, but the slaves think no different of them.)

Hrungnir: "All right, everyone! Back to work!"

(The slaves immediately run off to their posts, and resume digging. Hrungnir turns to the two overseers.)

Hrungnir: "I believe we just solved both of your problems. As you were, soldiers."

Scene 2: Wutai

(Setting: A village on the Far Eastern Continent. Strangely shaped buildings made of stone and wood fill the area. There are multi storied pagodas, statues, and other tall buildings. A river runs through the village, and a wooden bridge is connecting both sides. The buildings are painted a variety of bright colors. There are stone roads running throughout the village. Most of the people are inside because of the approaching night, and the bad weather. It is late in the evening. The scene takes place at the barracks while the sun is nearly set. The commander of the barracks is standing on the top floor of the pagoda. He is looking out over the southern ocean from the third story balcony. He leans forward on the wooden rail, a troubled expression on his face. The balcony doors are open behind him, and a light wind is blowing against his gray hair, and navy blue robe. The old man has been the sole commander of Wutai for many years now, and his face shows it. The scene begins as an armored warrior approaches him from inside the building.)

Warrior: (Bows.) "Sir!"

Commander: (Without moving from his position.) "What news do you bring, Kenshi?"

Kenshi: "The battle between the kingdoms has ended for now. Both sides have returned to their castles, and are currently looking to rebuild, and recover."

Commander: "There will be many more to come. It's only a matter of time."

Kenshi: "How can you be so sure?"

Commander: "History has a way of repeating itself. Men fail to learn from their past mistakes, and this is the result. Come. Join me on the railing, and let us enjoy the gentle night air."

Kenshi: (Walks over to the railing, and rests his arms against it.) "Sir, don't you think it is time for Wutai to choose a side? Surely we can't avoid this war entirely. Eventually one of the kingdoms will triumph over the other."

Commander: "We cannot have both peace, and power. The others have always desired power, while Wutai alone seeks peace. Our kingdom has always been a nation of separation. We have managed to stay out of the affairs of the rest of the world since the beginning. To change that now would be a grave mistake."

Kenshi: "I don't mean to argue, sir. What I have seen and heard within Stephis, however, brings me great torment. It causes me to fear for the future of Wutai."

Commander: "Come. Gaze out over the southern sea with me. Tell me what it is you see."

Kenshi: (Looks out into the distance.) "It's very dark out there. As dark as night. And the storm clouds are many."

Commander: "Yes. There is indeed a storm brewing to the south. While the two great kingdoms war with each other, a new storm is rising. One like none I have ever seen."

Kenshi: "Should we be worried?"

Commander: (Smiles.) "Wise men need not fear. But an intelligent man would prepare just the same."

Kenshi: "What shall I tell the spies to do next?"

Commander: "Have them continue to remain at their posts in Stephis and Lindsea. What they learn for us there is most important."

Kenshi: "And Amanda? Shall we continue to track her?"

Commander: "From afar, yes. But do not interfere. I wish to see what part she plays in this war. I find her choices as of late to be rather interesting."

Kenshi: (Bows.) "As you wish."

(The commander watches as Kenshi returns inside, and disappears. He turns his gaze back out over the ocean. He can feel the wind starting to pick up a little against his robe, while a single flash of lightning appears out in the distance. The commander watches on with great interest.)

Commander: "How many years has it been since we saw the last great typhoon?"

Scene 3: Stephis Castle

(Setting: At the top of the walls of Stephis Castle. It is night time, and a few guards are patrolling the top walkway. They are spaced out a lot, and there are torches lit up along the sides. The full moon shines brightly in the sky on this now cloudless night. Most of the soldiers are currently asleep in the castle, while others are in their houses in the town. Those that are awake are patrolling the top walls, and the front gate. There are also pairs of guards making their rounds inside all parts of the castle interior. Two grappling hooks suddenly appear over the wall, and they both attach themselves to the side. A few minutes later, one of the guards heads over toward them. He doesn't notice them in the darkness, but thinks he sees something odd. The scene begins when the guard comes over to investigate.)

Guard 1: (Notices the hooks on the wall.) "What do we have here?"

Pirate 1: (Whispers to Bart while holding on to the rope attached to one of the hooks.) "There's a guy above you! There's a guy above you!"

Bart: (Reaches up over the ledge, and grabs ahold of the guard. He pulls him over the edge, and watches as he falls down to the ground.)

Pirate 1: (When he hears the landing thud.) "There's a guy below you! There's a guy below you!"

Bart: "Arrr!"

(Bart and the other pirate climb up over the ledge, and stand up on the walkway. They check out the scene, and look ahead across the wall. They see the other pirate pair appear on top of the wall as well, along with the other guards that are patrolling their areas.)

Pirate 1: "Where to, captain?"

Bart: "We have to find a way in here, Smitty. Don't want to attract too much attention now. We keep to the shadows. Stay out of the light."

Smitty: "Aye."

(Bart leads the way along the wall, with Smitty right behind him. They try to avoid appearing in the moonlight, but there are fiery torches all over as well. Luckily, there are various objects sitting around that provide decent hiding spots. While Bart crouches behind some barrels, a guard walks right by him. The man turns to look at Bart in surprise.)

Guard 2: "What the?"

Bart: (Lunges forward with his cutlass, jabbing it right through him.) "Arrr!"

(Bart walks the guard toward the edge, and pushes him over with his foot. His sword exits his body, and the man falls to the ground. He lands with a thud.)

Smitty: (Stands up from behind a crate.) "That was a close one."

Bart: "Aye. Just have to hope nobody discovers the bodies. At least not until morning."

(Bart and Smitty continue along the wall. The other group went off in the other direction earlier, and as far as they know they are still making their way around. Bart notices a tower in the distance, and figures that to be the way in.)

Bart: "Avast!"

Smitty: (Stops.) "Hold it there, captain. Check this out."

(Bart turns around, and sees Smitty standing over a treasure chest. It was hidden behind some crates and barrels on the side. He walks over to it with his sword drawn.)

Bart: "Well what have we here? A rather strange place to keep this."

Smitty: "Could it be?"

Bart: (Slowly opens up the chest.) "Smitty! We've done it! We found the treasure!"

Smitty: (Looks at the tiny collection of gold necklaces, and jewels.) "Aye. A small part of course. But where is the rest of it?"

Bart: "If they left this one sitting up here all alone, then surely there must be more like this all over the castle. Smitty! Put these inside your sack, and let us continue on."

Smitty: "With pleasure, captain."

~~~~~~~~~~

In another part of the castle...

Pirate 1: "Arrr! Another chest!"

Pirate 2: "Quickly! Empty it out into your sack before someone sees us!"

Pirate 1: "Aye."

(The two pirates put the gold coins and jewels into their sacks, but leave the chest lid open. This way they will know they have already been here. The castle is a huge place, and they are both currently on the top floor. But that is as far as they know. Without a map to go by, they have no idea where they are.)

Pirate 1: "Where to?"

Pirate 2: "Let's just keep on in this direction, and work our way down. We have to find a way to open the gates so the others can enter."

Pirate 1: "Aye."

(The pirates make their way down the stone hallway. The entire castle is made of stone, and the hallways are lined with flaming torches along the walls. They try to avoid the light, but the floors have different crates and barrels sitting around on the sides to work around. As the pirates discover more chests, they make sure to empty the contents quickly before moving forward.)

Pirate 2: "Keep a lookout for more guards. They can be anywhere."

(They pass by closed wooden doors on either side as they go, until they approach another staircase. They can't tell if this is the same tower staircase they used before or not.)

Pirate 1: "Going down."

(The two start down the stone steps, but pause when they hear footsteps coming up. It sounds like more guards. The pirates turn around, and head back up to where they came from. They hope to hide behind some crates to create an ambush, but instead run into two more guards passing by in the hallway. The four men all see each other at once, and pull out their swords. The pirates already had their cutlasses out, which are naturally faster anyway.)

Pirate 1: "Arrr!"

(The pirates attack the surprised guards, and are able to take them down quickly. The two guards coming up the stairs hear the commotion, and appear at the top. They too are surprised, and take out their swords.)

Guard 1: "Halt! Who are you?"

Pirate 2: "That be none of your concern."

(The pirates attack, and take the first guard down. The second one pulls out a whistle, and sounds the alarm. It lets out a shrill sound, which alerts the entire castle to the intruders. The pirates continue to attack with their swords, causing the guard to fall. He hits the stone steps, his metal armor causing him to bounce farther down, which only adds to the noise. The two pirates look at each other.)

Pirate 1: "What are the chances nobody heard that?"

~~~~~~~~~~

Outside the castle gates...

(The two pirates watch the guards from their position in the bushes. They have been hiding here as they wait for the opportune moment to move. Whether the gates are opened by the other pirates inside, or by the guards on the outside, it makes no difference to them. They are determined to get inside by any means possible.)

Pirate 1: "What's that sound?"

(They listen as they hear several whistling sounds coming from the castle. It seems to be coming from inside, although it soon spreads to the guards on the outside as well. Once the two guards outside are done using their whistles, they run over to the gates, and open them up. The pirates watch with excitement, and uncertainty, as they see their chance to move.)

Pirate 2: (Stands up.) "This is it! Let's go!"

Pirate 1: (Pulls him back down.) "Hold it! There's more of them!"

(The two duck back down in the bushes, and watch as more guards emerge from inside the castle. There are six of them now, and they are all talking amongst themselves. Four men run back inside the castle, while the original two resume their posts by the now open gates. They make no effort to close them, and the whistling can still be heard coming from inside the castle.)

Pirate 2: "What do we do now?"

Pirate 1: "Keep to the plan. We're going in."

Scene 4: Stephis Castle

(Setting: The throne room in Stephis Castle. King Edward and Nichols are sitting on two separate thrones in the middle of the room. There is a long red carpet going from the front door of the room, all the way up to Edward's throne. There are two guards standing on either side of the doorway, both inside and outside the room. There are several exotic plants and animals in the huge throne room, with many animals currently sleeping. It is night time, and torches are burning along the walls. There are two large open windows on the wall behind the thrones, and the moonlight is shining through. The scene begins when a guard enters the room, and walks up to the thrones.)

Guard: (Bows.) "Majesty."

Edward: "Report."

Guard: "Sire. The alarm has been sound. We have reason to believe there are intruders inside the castle."

Nichols: "Have they been spotted?"

Guard: "Not yet. There was an attack on the upper levels of the castle. One guard managed to blow his whistle before he fell. When we arrived to investigate, we found four downed guards lying there. The invaders must still be inside somewhere."

Edward: "Lindsea soldiers?"

Nichols: "Not likely. Not after that last battle. Lindsea was badly damaged. There's no way they decided to attack us so soon."

Edward: "Then who could it be?"

Nichols: "It has to be Thomas. He has come to rescue the princess. No other person alive would dare such a feat."

Edward: "That is mighty bold of him. Does he have a death wish? Breaking into Stephis Castle, and attacking our men?"

Nichols: "Where is the princess now?"

Guard: "I believe she is currently in one of the town prisons. She left the castle dungeon not too long ago."

Nichols: "Find her, and bring her to us. Thomas must not be

allowed to free her yet again."

Guard: (Bows.) "Yes, my lord."

Edward: "Alert the other soldiers as well. Daevas included. I want every man on duty, and I want the entire remaining army ready for battle."

Guard: "What should I tell them?"

Edward: "Tell them that a great threat to the kingdom is somewhere in our midst, and must be stopped. I want soldiers all over the castle, and the town as well. Anyone who is not a citizen of Stephis, or appears suspicious in any way, is to be killed immediately. That includes all prisoners as well."

Guard: "All of them?"

Edward: "All of them."

Nichols: "He's right. Many of our prisoners came from Lindsea. We can't afford to leave anyone alive who will help either Thomas or Mary. They must all be put to death. The alternative is that the prisoners are released, and be made to fight against us alongside Thomas and Mary. This also cannot be."

Edward: "I never considered that one. We definitely don't need Thomas building up an army in our midst. The prisoners must die. Do you understand?"

Guard: "Yes, sir!"

Edward: "Good. Then get to work."

(Edward and Nichols watch as the guard leaves the throne room. They then turn to each other to consider what else they can do.)

Edward: "This could be it. This is our chance to finally put an end to Thomas. If we send the entire army out after him, there's no way he can survive."

Nichols: "You're right. We need to find Mary as well. It may be that we can use her to get to him. Or at least convince him to surrender, and turn himself in. Either way, Thomas dies tonight."

Edward: "Funny how things work out these days. We didn't even have to do a thing. Thomas has come straight to us."

Nichols: (Stands up.) "I must go now. I need to prepare for battle. If this is our chance to end it all, I want to see that it happens."

Edward: "Then I will stay here, and wait for further reports."

Nichols: (As he heads toward the doors.) "I shall return shortly."

Scene 5: Stephis Town

(Setting: It is still night in Stephis town. Clouds have reappeared, and are blocking out the moonlight at times as they move. The town itself is about medium size. Not nearly as big as Lindsea, but much bigger than the others on the Western Continent. Stephis is a battle centered kingdom, and it shows. The town is a mix of houses and stores, but most of the buildings are for training, and weapon storage. There are multiple barracks, archery ranges, stables, and siege workshops. There are a few weapon stores, magic shops, and item shops. There are also numerous prisons, along with the discreetly hidden monster factory. Most of the buildings are made of bricks, but the houses are made of sticks and stones. The whole town is made up of brick roads and pathways. There are some farms and mills on the outside of town, along with some mining camps closer to the mountains. A lumber mill is near the woods as well. The castle can be seen to the north of town. There are burning torches along the roads, and near the doors of the buildings. Cid and Amanda are sneaking through the shadows to the next prison. They are still wearing the Stephis armor they found earlier. Scene begins when they spot the two guards standing outside a small unremarkable building, with barred windows.)

Cid: "I've been thinking. We don't have to sneak around here anymore since we have the armor on. It only seems more suspicious that way."

Amanda: "That's a good point. Guess I'll never get used to just walking through the streets of Stephis. But we can try it if you think it's ok."

Cid: "I do."

(Cid and Amanda step out of the shadows, and onto the stone road. They walk normally toward the prison, and approach the two guards. The guards salute them, and they attempt to repeat the same back to them.)

Guard 1: "What news do you bring?"

Cid: "We've been sent to relieve you. Command wants to switch things up a bit tonight."

Guard 2: "Is that so? This is the first we've heard of it."

Cid: "It is. Apparently there are some important prisoners being held in Stephis right now. They want to make sure to switch guards pretty regularly."

Guard 1: "Well, if that's what they want to do. Where should we report to?"

Amanda: "They need to see you at the castle. Pronto."

Guard 2: "I hate when they do this to us."

Guard 1: "Yeah. They never tell us anything. Here."

(The guard hands Cid the keys to the prison. Amanda and Cid take over the post as the two guards start walking back to the castle. They wait a little while until they are out of sight before they start talking.)

Amanda: "I wonder how long we can keep this up."

Cid: "Long enough to find Mary I hope. Let's do this."

(Cid hands Amanda the keys. She turns around, and tries out each one until she finds the key that fits the door. When it finally unlocks, she opens it up, and they both look inside the dark building.)

Amanda: "Here goes nothing."

~~~~~~~~~~

In another part of town...

Dustin: "There's another one."

Thomas: "How many prisons are in this town?"

Dustin: "A lot, apparently."

(Thomas and Dustin make their way toward the brick building. They see the two guards standing outside the front door. Dustin still looks a little suspicious with his poorly fitting armor, but they have been fine so far. He doesn't remember each prison having two guards when he worked here, but times are changing. Mary is trapped in one of them, so that probably has something to do with it.)

Thomas: (While walking along the road.) "Try to act normal."

Dustin: "When do I not?"

Guard 1: (Eyes Dustin suspiciously.) "Can we help you fellas?"

Dustin: "Yeah. We were just coming over to relieve you for a break."

Guard 2: "But we just got back from break."

Thomas: "Are you sure about that? Cause they told us specifically to come to this prison."

Guard 1: "They must have told you wrong."

Thomas: "We have a lot of extra help tonight because of the situation." (Shrugs.) "Maybe they just want you to have another break."

Guard 2: "I don't know about this. Something doesn't seem

right. We never even get to have one break."

Dustin: "I would just go on break, and take it up with the boss later. If it were me. If we leave now, we won't back again later tonight."

Guard 1: "Maybe we should do it. The chances of this happening again are nearly impossible."

Guard 2: "I'm still not convinced. Before we give you the keys, answer this question. Who is the General of the Stephis army?"

Thomas: "Um..."

Dustin: "General... Parker?"

Guard 2: (Hands Dustin the keys.) "Ok. Here you go."

(Dustin takes the keys, and the two guards step away from their posts. Thomas and Dustin take their place as the guards start to walk back to the castle. Suddenly, the two men turn around, and pull out their swords.)

Guard 2: "You're not real guards! Who are you?"

Thomas: (Takes out his sword.) "Looks like the jig is up."

Dustin: (Pulls out his axe.) "Oh well. You win some, you lose some."

(The guards come at Thomas and Dustin with their swords. Thomas trades blows with his own sword, while Dustin attacks with the axe. Dustin adds in a thunder spell that hits both men with lightning.)

Guard 1: (Surprised.) "Magic? Who are you?"

Thomas: "Wouldn't you like to know."

(Dustin uses another thunder spell, and Thomas hits the last guard with his sword. When both men are down, they turn their attention back to the prison.)

Dustin: "Well that didn't go so bad."

Thomas: "We definitely almost had em."

Dustin: (While putting the key in the lock.) "I sure hope she's in this one."

Thomas: "Me too, D. Me too."

~~~~~~~~~~

A little later... in another prison...

(Mary tosses and turns on the rough straw bed as she tries to get comfortable. She is having a hard time sleeping tonight, and even when she does, her mind is troubled by countless nightmares. She finally opens her eyes, and stares up at the dark prison ceiling. It takes her a little to remember where she is through all the dreams. She looks across the room, and sees Doctor Tot snoring up against the wall. She can't help but feel bad for him. He was almost like a father to her growing up, and now he is forced to live the rest of his life as a prisoner of Stephis.)

Mary: (Sighs.)

(Mary turns her eyes toward the door as she hears a key inside the lock. The door opens up, and in walks what must be Stephis soldiers. One man is holding a fiery torch, while another carries a sword. They don't speak, but immediately get to work. The torch holder stands in the middle of the prison to light it up, while the other man walks over to Tot. With his sword in his hand, the soldier jabs the blade straight through the old man's heart. Tot opens his eyes in surprise, and soon after breathes his last breath. The soldier removes his sword, and turns to face Mary.)

Mary: (While standing up.) "NNNNNNNOOOOOO!!!"

Soldier 1: (Approaches Mary's cell.) "It's time to move, princess. Orders are orders."

Mary: "What have you done? How could you do such a thing?"

Soldier 2: "The king has ordered us to kill all prisoners. Just be glad you are the exception."

Mary: "No! You can't do that to me! You can't do that to them! They don't deserve this!"

Soldier 1: "I'm sorry. It's just the way it is."

(Suddenly, a ball of fire flies through the open doorway, and hits the soldier holding the torch. The other one looks at him in shock as he gets hit too. An arrow follows the fireball, and hits the guy with the torch, taking him down. The last soldier starts walking toward the door with his sword ready, but also gets attacked by an arrow. The man falls to the ground, and doesn't get back up.)

Mary: "Now what? A monster attack?"

(Mary watches as two new Stephis soldiers walk into the prison. She backs away in fear as she sees the bow in the hands of one of them. The soldiers look around the room at the carnage, then over at Mary. She is a little confused at what's happening, because it almost seems like two Stephis soldiers just killed two other Stephis soldiers, but that doesn't make any sense to her. The two new guys don't say anything, but one of them bends down to take the prison keys off of one of the downed guards, while the other picks up the torch. They then turn to face Mary, and both remove their helmets at the same time. Mary's mouth drops open in disbelief when she sees their faces in the fire.)

Mary: "Amanda? Cid?"

Amanda: "Miss us?"

Cid: "You have no idea how hard it is to find a person in this town. We were just starting to lose hope here."

Mary: (Starts to cry.) "Is it really you? I can't believe it! I thought you were Stephis soldiers."

Amanda: (Takes off her armor, and drops it on the ground.) "It's really us. That feels so much better."

Cid: (Removes his armor as well.) "What do you say we get you out of here, and go back to Lindsea?"

Mary: (With tears in her eyes.) "That sounds amazing."

(Amanda unlocks the door, and Mary immediately throws her arms around her. She hugs Cid next, then wipes her eyes clean.)

Mary: "Is Thomas here? And Dustin?"

Cid: "They're here too. We've been looking all over for you. You won't believe what happened."

Mary: "You'll have to tell me everything."

Cid: "We will. But first, let's get you out of here. We have to find the others, and escape before morning."

Mary: "I'm afraid I lost my staff. I think it's still inside the castle dungeon. They moved me so many times. We have to go back for it."

Amanda: "Leave it to me. I'll get you in there."

(The three start toward the open doorway, but Mary stops, and heads over to Doctor Tot. She kneels down in front of him, and watches him quietly. Cid notices her there, and turns back around.)

Cid: "What's wrong?"

Mary: (With tears coming down her cheeks.) "He was like a father to me, and they killed him. For no good reason."

Amanda: "Who is he?"

Mary: "Doctor Tot. He taught me everything when I was little. And now he's gone."

Cid: "I'm sorry, Mary. It's just another reason why we have to end this war."

(Amanda and Cid are puzzled to see Mary reach inside Tot's robes. She searches around a little, and finally pulls out the diamond bracer. She climbs back up to her feet, and turns toward Cid.)

Mary: "Doctor Tot sacrificed his life for this. I need you to hold on to it for me."

Cid: (Takes the bracer, and puts it on his forearm.) "Sure, Mary. Whatever you need."

Mary: "I also have to finish what he started. But not now. First thing we need to work on is getting out of here."

Amanda: "So what are we waiting for? Let's go!"

Act 5: THE PROTECTOR

Scene 1: Stephis Castle

(Setting: The inside halls of Stephis Castle. The walls, floor, and ceiling are all made of stone. There are burning torches spaced out along the walls, and at times a closed wooden door as well. Crates, barrels, and an occasional treasure chest sit in random locations. Pairs of guards are patrolling the entire castle, but they are all armed, and ready for combat. The intruder alarm has already been sound, and all guards are on the lookout for anyone who doesn't belong. It is still night time, and the pirate pairs are making their way around. The scene begins with Bart and Smitty by an open chest.)

Bart: (Puts $200 gil inside his sack.) "Another chest found."

Smitty: "Where to, captain?"

Bart: "We must find the treasury."

(Bart and Smitty sneak through the stone castle halls. After a while everything begins to look the same to them. The halls are cluttered with various crates and barrels, along with an occasional chest. They provide good hiding places if needed, but they also slow the pirates down. The burning torches along the walls provide some light, but mostly just shadows bouncing around. They have no idea where they are, or where they are going. All they know is that there are several floors to the castle, and they must make their way down. The treasure room is somewhere in this huge place. They are sure that the castle gates are on the bottom level, and that's going to be their escape route. Supposing they can stay alive long enough to get there.)

Smitty: (Stops.) "Guards ahead."

(Two guards make their way down the hall toward the pirates. Their swords are out, and one of them is blowing his whistle. Bart and Smitty draw their swords, and move up to meet them.)

Guard 1: "Halt, intruders! What is your business here?"

Bart: "Our business is none of your business!"

Guard 1: "Then prepare to die!"

(The two pairs trade blows with their swords. The pirate cutlasses are smaller, and quicker than the long swords used by the guards. The pirates lack in armor though, and don't carry a huge shield to block hits with. It doesn't take long for the guards to go down, but Smitty takes a good bit of damage during the battle.)

Bart: "Are you going to make it?"

Smitty: "Aye. Nothing a good potion or two won't fix."

~~~~~~~~~~

Elsewhere in the castle...

Pirate 1: "My sack is filling up. We might need to go unload some of this back at camp before long."

Pirate 2: "Aye. We haven't even found the treasury yet. I still have room in mine though."

(The pirates make their way through a different part of the castle. They are on a lower level, but they still aren't sure where. They hesitate to go inside any of the closed wooden doors, but they are sure that one of them has to be the treasure room. Most of the doors are locked anyway, and none give any hint to what might be inside.)

Pirate 1: "I wonder how all the others are doing."

Pirate 2: "There's no telling. Me thinks this is a mighty dangerous mission here. It's hard enough trying to take back the treasure, but then we have to rescue this princess lady too. And with the whole Stephis army out there."

Pirate 1: "Aye. It be a miracle if we make it out of here alive."

(The pirates continue down the hall, until they spot a pair of guards up ahead. They turn around to go back to the shadows, but stop when a door opens up in front of them. Two more guards emerge, and immediately blow their whistles.)

Guard 1: "Intruders!"

Guard 2: "Get them!"

Pirate 1: "Arrr!"

(The two guards trade sword blows with the pirates. The pair of guards in the distance notice the battle, and blow their whistles as well. They take out their swords, and make their way down the hall. By the time they arrive, the other two guards are down, but the two pirates have also taken damage.)

Guard 3: (When he approaches the pirates.) "Halt!"

Pirate 2: "More of them?"

(The two pirates focus their attacks on the first guard to take him down. When there is only one left, they both turn to face him.)

Pirate 1: "Three down, one to go."

Guard 4: "Is that so?"

Pirate 2: "Arrr!"

(The two pirates watch in amazement as the last guard begins to change. His entire skin turns red, and his body starts to bob and bounce around. He looks like a red blob of jelly.)

Pirate 1: "What is that?"

Pirate 2: "I've never seen anything like it. A monster soldier?"

Guard 4: "Consider me your first and last fire flan."

Pirate 1: "?!"

(The monster launches a ball of fire toward the two pirates. It hits both of them, causing one to go down. The other is damaged, but unwilling to give up just yet.)

Pirate 1: "What power is this?"

(The pirate attacks with his sword, but the blade just bounces off the blob. He stares at him in shock when he realizes that his weapon can't hurt him.)

Flan: (Prepares to cast fire again.) "I hope you like your meat well done."

~~~~~~~~~~

Later...

Bart: "Another staircase. Going down."

(Bart and Smitty head down the winding tower steps. They

end up on another floor that looks just like the floors above them. They both glance at each other, and continue on.)

Smitty: "How much farther to the treasure room, do you think?"

Bart: "I don't know. But my sack still has plenty of space. It must be close though. I can feel it."

Smitty: "You did choose the biggest sack we had, captain."

Bart: "Aye. The captain always carries the biggest sack."

Smitty: "Aye."

(The men pause when they hear the thud. They listen as it continues to repeat itself. They can feel the stone floor beneath them rumbling a little with each additional thud.)

Smitty: "What do you suppose that is?"

(Bart and Smitty watch as a giant figure moves toward them from down the hall. He looks like a guard, but this one is much taller than the others. He also carries a great axe on his shoulder. Each time the man steps forward, the pirates hear the sound, and feel the ground shake below. They pull out their swords, and prepare for battle.)

Smitty: "It's just a guard."

Bart: "I don't think this is an ordinary guard. Look at him."

(As the man approaches, they can see what he really looks like. His arms and legs are huge, along with the rest of his body. It appears that his muscles are bulging out of his armor. His skin is a tan color, not like that of the other guards. Bart immediately knows something is off here.)

Bart: "What are you?"

Guard: "When humans fail to stop intruders, they send a golem to get the job done."

Bart: "Stephis is using monsters as soldiers now? Interesting."

Smitty: "What do we do, captain?"

Bart: "Take him down."

(The pirates attack quickly with their swords, but the golem is strong. It takes many hits to hurt the beast. The golem himself is slow, but powerful. He attempts to swing at Bart with his axe, but Bart easily dodges the blow. After a few failed attempts to hit the men, the golem puts the axe away on his back.)

Golem: (Raises his huge fists.) "Now it's time to bring the pain."

(The golem lunges for Bart, but misses. He ends up hitting the wall, which breaks off some of the stone. The clay that makes up the golem's fist crumbles as well, turning to dust as it falls.)

Smitty: "He's made of clay!"

Bart: "Aye. Keep up the attack!"

(The pirates continue to slice at the golem. Each cut causes pieces of clay to fall off the monster. The golem finally manages to punch Smitty, knocking him back into the wall.)

Smitty: (Shakes his head.) "I don't think I can handle anymore of that."

Golem: "There's much more where that came from."

(The battle continues, and all three fighters are wearing down. The golem is coming apart, and the pirates are even more sure of victory. As the golem is about to fall, he hits Smitty with one final blow. Smitty flies backward down the hall, and lands with a thud. Bart delivers the final blows, slicing through the legs of the golem. The remainder of his body crashes to the floor, shaking the whole place.)

Bart: "Smitty!"

(Bart runs over to his fallen partner, and sees that he isn't going to get up this time. He shakes his head, and takes Smitty's treasure sack from him. He empties it out into his own, and drops the bag on the floor.)

Bart: "You fought well, my friend. May your death not be in vain."

(Bart turns back around, and continues on down the hallway.)

Scene 2: Stephis Castle

(Setting: Inside the castle dungeon. The stone dungeon is cold, damp, and dark. Some torches are burning along the walls, but a lot of them have run out. It is eerily quiet at the moment, but it's also very late at night. There are cells all over the place, and rusty chains attached to multiple walls. Small puddles of water are all over. Most prisoners are assumed to be asleep at the moment. A key can be heard being put inside the front door. The door is unlocked, and slowly opened up. In walks Amanda, Cid, and Mary into the dungeon. Cid carries a burning torch. They close the door behind them, and turn to face the dungeon.)

Cid: "Is this it?"

Mary: "It has to be."

Amanda: "Those guards didn't put up much of a fight. They practically handed us the keys."

Cid: "That's only because we got the drop on them. They never even saw us coming."

Amanda: "That's true."

Mary: "My staff has to be around here somewhere. I think they dropped it on the floor somewhere when they brought me here. I just hope someone didn't take it with them."

Cid: "Let's hope not. We still have to find the others, and get out of here."

Amanda: "What about the prisoners? What should we do with them?"

Mary: "I wish we could save them all. I just don't know how to get them all out of here. There is one here though that I have to find. I promised her that I would get her out of here."

Amanda: "We should have the keys at least. Let's look around."

(The group separates, and searches around for Mary's staff. Amanda casts fire on the unlit torches to make more light. Mary also looks for Harriet as well, and is pretty sure she is in the same cell as before. She knows it will be hard to get her out of here now, but it's a chance she is willing to take. It looks like all the prisoners are asleep, and the party begins to wonder if they are also on the king's kill list. As Cid peers into a cell with his torch, his foot slips over something on the floor. He looks down, and picks up Mary's staff.)

Cid: "I found it!"

(Mary comes over to him, and reclaims her staff. She runs her hands along it to clean it off, then examines the white Krystal on top.)

Mary: "Yes!"

Amanda: "Prison break time?"

Mary: "Help me find Harriet, you guys."

(The three head over to the cells in the back. Mary thinks she finds the right one, and can see Harriet sleeping inside. Amanda tries the keys until she finds the one that opens the door. Once open, Mary heads inside to wake her.)

Mary: (Shakes Harriet.) "Wake up. It's me, Mary. I've come to get you out of here."

(Mary tries to wake Harriet up, but she doesn't budge. Cid brings the torch closer to see if it helps. Mary manages to turn her over on her back, only to realize the truth.)

Mary: "No! Not you too!"

Amanda: "What is it? What's wrong?"

Mary: "They've already been here! She's dead! They're probably all dead!"

Cid: "We're too late."

Amanda: "Let's check the other cells. See if anyone else is still alive."

(The three separate once more, checking on a number of prisoners in the dungeon. Sure enough, the soldiers have already been here.)

Mary: "I can't believe it! Why? How could they do this?"

Amanda: "Because this is how they are. What they do. They're all a bunch of monsters."

Cid: "Come on, guys. There's nothing more we can do here."

(The three sadly make their way back to the front door. They stop when they see it opening up from the outside. They prepare their weapons, and wait to see who comes in. A lone guard walks into the dungeon, and spots the party. He closes the door behind him, and snorts.)

Guard: "Finally! Some action!"

Cid: "You got a lot of nerve killing a bunch of innocent prisoners."

Mary: "You should be ashamed of yourself!"

Guard: "Ashamed? I think not. This is what I was made to do."

Amanda: "Made?"

(The party watches as the guard grows in size. His skin turns green, and his neck lengthens. A long tail appears behind him, along with sharp teeth and claws. Two wings also appear behind his back. The green dragon snorts at the party once more.)

Amanda: "Not this again!"

Green Dragon: "I think it's time for a snack!"

Cid: (Prepares a poison arrow.) "Snack on this!"

(Cid shoots his arrow, which poisons the dragon. Amanda tries an ice spell, while the dragon attacks with his claws. His attacks are strong, and Mary has to heal Amanda immediately. The dragon sticks to physical attacks, while Cid uses his arrows, and Amanda uses magic. Mary tries to keep everyone healthy.)

Green Dragon: "Nobody leaves this dungeon alive!"

Amanda: (Runs over, and attacks with her daggers.) "Speak for yourself!"

(The dragon whips Mary with his tail, and Amanda cures her. Cid tries a darkness arrow to blind the beast.)

Green Dragon: "What is this?!"

Mary: "This is your end! Keep it up, team!"

(The three continue their attacks as the dragon wears down. He misses most of his hits now, but they are still strong when they do connect. A little while longer, and the dragon finally falls.)

Amanda: "All right!"

Cid: "Let's stop playing around, and get out of here."

Scene 3: Stephis Town

(Setting: Near a prison in the middle of Stephis town. It is still dark outside, and the full moon is shining bright. There is a lot of activity for this hour of the night. Stephis soldiers are everywhere right now, and the citizens are being kept inside their homes. The soldiers are searching the whole town for anyone not belonging to Stephis. They have already killed most of the prisoners, and there are only a few jails left to visit. Dead soldiers and pirates are scattered throughout town from various battles. All of the pirates who were assigned to the town are now dead. The scene begins with Thomas and Dustin heading for another prison. They are still wearing their disguises from earlier, and have had little trouble passing as Stephis soldiers.)

Dustin: "It's starting to get pretty busy around here."

Thomas: "Yeah. It's not making our job any easier. Let's just hope these disguises hold up."

(Thomas and Dustin make their way over to the prison. The two guards standing there notice them right away.)

Guard 1: "It's about time you guys got here. We could use a break. All these people out here, and everyone is too busy for us."

Thomas: "Guess it's your lucky day. What's going on here anyway?"

Guard 2: "The king has ordered all prisoners to be killed. He also woke up the whole Stephis army, and put them to work. Apparently there are some suspicious characters running around here causing trouble. I can't imagine anyone crazy enough to do that, but I guess the times are changing."

Dustin: "Have you seen anyone suspicious around here?"

Guard 2: "Not yet. Anyway, here are the keys. We'll be back soon."

(Dustin takes the keys, and he and Thomas switch spots with the two guards. They watch them walk off before they start talking again.)

Thomas: "Mary…"

Dustin: "Do they know we're here? Did the others get

caught?"

Thomas: "I don't know. But we need to see if Mary is in here."

(Dustin unlocks the door, and he and Thomas enter the prison. This one actually has three cells, and is slightly larger than the last few have been. They both check over the whole place, and find nothing but three dead prisoners inside. Mary isn't here.)

Thomas: "Well it's good that she's not here, but then we still don't know where she is. There can't be that many prisons left around here. Right?"

Dustin: "Between us and the others, we must have checked them all by now."

Thomas: "So where is she? Did they move her somewhere? Is she in the castle? Is she even alive?"

Dustin: "I don't know. I really don't."

Thomas: (Frustrated.) "We're running out of time. All these soldiers out here aren't helping either. What if the others get caught? Or worse? We'll have to save them too."

Dustin: "If they are going around and killing all the prisoners, then we can probably forget about setting them free."

Thomas: "I just want to get Mary out of here. I know that sounds bad, but that's what we came here for. She's the only one I care about."

Dustin: "I know. Why don't we just head over to the castle? As long as they think we are soldiers we can go anywhere. Besides, the dungeon there is huge. If they had to pick one place to keep her, that would be it."

Thomas: "We are supposed to stay in the town. But I guess the situation is changing. Ok. Let's go."

(Thomas and Dustin exit the prison, and close the door behind them. Dustin drops the keys on the ground since there is no point to keeping them. They follow the road up to the castle, and after a while come across some fallen soldiers in the street. They inspect the scene, and notice the two pirates laying there as well.)

Dustin: "This isn't a good sign."

(They make sure nobody else is around, then pick up the sacks that the pirates had on them, and sling them on their backs. They can feel some treasure inside each one.)

Thomas: "I've got a bad feeling about this."

Scene 4: Stephis Castle

(Setting: The treasury inside Stephis Castle. It is early morning now, and still dark outside. Bart is rummaging around by himself inside the huge stone room. There are all sorts of valuables in here. Pieces of gold, silver, jewels, and Gil are scattered all over. Nothing is organized at all. It's just a random collection of treasures from all over the world. The room is full of treasure chests, jewelry, pottery, weapons, armor, brightly colored stones, animal skins, furs, and even fancy outfits. Bart makes his way around with his sack, trying to pick out the things he wants, and anything that seems valuable. The walls of the treasury are covered in burning torches, and there are several on posts around the room. There is one set of double doors which lead back out to the castle hallway, and they are currently closed.

Scene begins with Bart putting some gold jewelry in his sack.)

Bart: "Obviously my first mistake here was not bringing a bigger sack. My second mistake of course was not bringing a bunch more sacks."

(Bart walks around picking up gold coins off the stone floor. He gathers up a number of them, then hears the treasury doors start to creak open. He sits the sack down, and takes out his sword. He watches as three figures make their way into the room, shutting the doors behind them.)

Cid: "There you are! We've been looking all over for you."

Bart: (Puts his sword away.) "Aye. It has been a long night. But I finally found it. The treasure."

Amanda: (With big eyes.) "Wow! So many shiny things!"

Cid: "I guess you found what you were looking for then."

Bart: "Aye. I might say the same for you too."

Amanda: "Yeah! We found her all right, but it wasn't easy."

Bart: "This must be the princess."

Mary: "You can call me Mary. And you are?"

Bart: "The name is Black Bart. Master of the high seas."

Mary: "Strange, I've not heard of you before."

Bart: "You didn't tell her?"

Amanda: (Shrugs.) "Been a little busy here."

Mary: "I take it you must be working with Lindsea, considering the situation here."

Bart: "Ahem. Black Bart serves no kingdom. I serve only freedom. It just so happens that your friends here were in need of saving you, and I was in need of reclaiming my treasure which was taken from me. So we struck a truce."

Mary: "I see. So what now?"

Bart: "Now we gather up as much as we can carry, and get ourselves back to the ship before the whole Stephis army comes after us. Which I think might be any minute now."

Cid: "Not everybody is going to make it back. We found a few pirates along the way that fell in battle."

Bart: "I know. I lost my partner too. But we've come this far. There's no quitting now."

(Bart hands Mary his extra sack, while Cid and Amanda take their sacks out.)

Bart: "We might not get away with all we could have, but anything is better than nothing at this point. Grab what you can, and let's get out of here."

(The four walk around the room, and fill their bags with everything that looks good. Cid catches Amanda stuffing some gold coins in her belt pouch, and just shakes his head.)

Cid: "Helping yourself are you?"

Amanda: "Why not? They won't miss it."

Bart: "Time is running out. Let's finish it up here."

(Everyone takes their sacks over to the doors, and notices that Amanda isn't with them. Cid spots her near a fancy looking treasure chest, and waves her over.)

Cid: "Come on!"

Amanda: "I just want to see what's in here!"

(Amanda opens up the lid, and a black mist comes out of the chest. She backs away as the mist fills the air around it. The others come closer to see what's going on. As the party stands there, they watch as the chest breaks apart into smaller wooden pieces. The mist rearranges the pieces into what looks like a figure. It has two arms, two legs, a head, a tail, and a body. When the mist finally settles, a monster of some sort is standing before the group.)

Cid: "What did you do this time?"

Amanda: "I didn't do anything! I just wanted to look!"

Bart: (Takes out his sword.) "It's a mimic. I've seen these before. They look like a chest, but transform into something else when you open them."

Mary: "What do we now?"

Bart: "We fight, and hope we can kill it."

Cid: "What do you mean hope?"

Bart: "Just hit it with everything you got!"

(Bart attacks the creature with his sword, while Cid uses his arrows. The mimic casts ice on the party in response. Mary heals them, while Amanda tries a fire spell.)

Amanda: "I don't think that did anything."

Bart: "Try another spell if you have one. Mimics are very specific in how they take damage. This one seems to be affected by weapons. It may be resistant to magic."

Amanda: "Well that sucks."

(The group keeps up the physical attacks while Mary heals. The mimic gets some strong magic damage in, and Amanda has to act as a backup healer. She tries an ice spell, but it doesn't do anything.)

Amanda: (Takes out her daggers.) "Guess it's slice and dice time!"

(The four work on the mimic with their weapons while the creature attacks with magic. It takes a while, but eventually the creature collapses into a puff of dust.)

Amanda: "We're gonna miss our ride out of here now."

Bart: "The ship never sails without the captain. Always remember that."

Scene 5: Stephis Castle

(Setting: Inside Stephis castle. Bart, Mary, Cid, and Amanda are racing for the castle gates with their sacks full of treasure. The sun will soon be rising, and they are trying to make their escape. They run into pairs of guards as they go, and have to take them down in order to move forward. They don't come across any other pirates, and assume them all to be dead. As for Thomas and Dustin, they see no signs of them either. The group fights their way forward through the stone halls, and eventually reaches the gates. They take down the two guards before they are able to shut the doors on them, and slip out into Stephis.)

Mary: "What do we do now?"

Bart: "We have to get back to camp, then make for the ship."

Mary: "But what about the others?"

Bart: "We keep to the code. Find the treasure, and get back to camp."

Mary: "But what about Thomas and Dustin?"

Bart: "They know the plan. Everyone has until morning to get back."

Mary: "Then what?"

Bart: "Anyone who falls behind stays behind."

Mary: (Stops moving, and folds her arms across her chest.) "I'm not leaving here without them."

Bart: "Suit yourself. I'm going back to camp. The whole Stephis army is out here looking for us right now. We won't last if we stand around here waiting."

(The party spots a group of soldiers heading their way. They take out their weapons, and immediately begin to fight them off. Once the soldiers are down, they pick up their sacks again to continue.)

Cid: "Hold on! There's more!"

(They watch as another group heads their way. As they prepare to deal with them, Amanda spots 2 more soldiers coming right behind them.)

Amanda: "Where are they all coming from?"

Cid: "It looks like the town. Everyone is heading back to the castle."

(The party fights off the two new groups, only to find another mass of soldiers heading their way. They look around for a way to escape, but find more soldiers coming from different directions. It's as if they are all coming right for them.)

Bart: "They're trying to surround us!"

Mary: "What do we do?"

(The party fights off any soldiers that get close to them, but the new ones are coming a lot faster than they can fight off. As the whole Stephis army begins to form a circle around the group, they notice the castle gates open up a little more. Out walks Nichols in his black robe. He is carrying his black staff, with the little black Krystal on top. He smiles as he makes his way toward the group.)

Nichols: "Oh, Mary. Did you really think you could escape me again? Escape the entire Stephis army? I think not."

Amanda: "I've got a few choice words for you, buster!"

Nichols: "My, my! What energy! It's a shame you all choose to fight against me. Just imagine the possibilities if we were all on the same side."

Mary: "We will never side with you, Nichols! Never!"

Nichols: "Yes, I know this is true. Unfortunate, but true. You really leave me no choice anymore."

(The circle around the group grows larger as the soldiers pack themselves in. There are about a hundred surrounding the party right now, and there is no way out. Nichols moves up to the party, and three soldiers join him. Everyone takes out their weapons, and prepares to fight.)

Nichols: "You cannot hope to win here, Mary. Today will be your last!"

(Nichols is interrupted as two Stephis soldiers push their way through the crowd. They finally break through, and join up with the party. Everyone stares at them in bewilderment.)

Nichols: "No matter. Defectors will be destroyed just as well."

(The two soldiers start to remove their armor, dropping each piece on the ground. When they're finished, everyone is shocked to see Thomas and Dustin standing there.)

Mary: (Her eyes grow wide with excitement.) "Thomas?"

Thomas: "You weren't about to face Nichols without us were you?"

Amanda: "We didn't seem to have much of a choice really."

Dustin: (Pulls out his axe.) "What do you say we finish him off, and get out of here?"

Amanda: "Yeah!"

Nichols: "Well then. Let's see what you got!"

(The party immediately starts the attack. Mary works on keeping everyone healthy, while the others attack with magic and weapons. Amanda helps heal as needed. The Stephis soldiers attack with their weapons and go down pretty easily, but as soon as one goes down, another steps in from the crowd to replace him. Nichols is the strongest one there, and hits the party with a variety of magic spells. All the soldiers surrounding the battle cheer every time Nichols casts a spell.)

Nichols: "Don't even think about running away either. None of you will leave here alive. Am I right, boys?"

(The soldiers in the audience laugh when Nichols speaks. Almost as if it were planned, a number of soldiers start to transform into their monster forms. They growl and roar at the party in an attempt to scare them.)

Amanda: (Sticks her tongue out at the monsters.) "You don't scare us!"

Nichols: "We'll see about that."

(The battle continues on. Nichols hits the party with his magic spells, causing Mary and Amanda to struggle to keep up with healing. Whenever a party member falls, Mary quickly uses the life spell. The group tries to focus on Nichols, but the soldiers are endless.)

Thomas: "Oh yeah! I've got a new spell to try out."

(Thomas casts haste on the group to speed them up, then the next chance he gets he tries out the stop spell. It doesn't affect Nichols at all, but the whole party watches in amazement as the three soldiers seem to freeze in place.)

Amanda: "Cool."

Nichols: "Somehow you still continue to amaze me. I offer you one last chance. Join me, or die."

Thomas: "Never!"

Nichols: "Have it your way."

(Nichols casts the flare spell, and the whole group is hit with the flame. Mary revives Amanda first, who brings Bart back with a phoenix down. Thomas and Cid toss a few potions around to try to heal everyone. Just as the party starts to recover, Nichols casts another flare spell. This time everyone goes down except for Dustin and Mary.)

Dustin: "We can't take much more of this!"

Nichols: What's the matter? Can't take the heat?"

(Mary and Dustin try to revive the group as fast as they can. When everyone is back up, the stop spell wears off, and the soldiers can move again.)

Amanda: "Ugh!"

Mary: "Hold on, guys!"

(Mary tries to cast shell on everyone, then protect as the soldiers begin their attacks again. Everyone turns to healing as more start to go down again.)

Mary: "Thomas!"

Nichols: "Not even Thomas can save you now! Flare!"

(The fireball hits the party once more, taking everyone down but Thomas and Mary. As they are both hunched over, the whole Stephis army cheers. Nichols smiles because he knows this is the end. As he prepares to cast flare one last time, Mary moves her hand up to the moonstone pendant around her neck. The yellow stone grows warm, and starts to shine beneath her fingers. She sees the bright light, and takes her hand away. Nichols watches in awe, and the army slowly quiets down as they begin to notice it too. The light continues to grow brighter until it finally covers the whole party.)

Nichols: "Now that's interesting."

(The bright yellow light continues to spread out from the party. It covers Nichols and the soldiers next, then moves over the army surrounding them. It grows so much that it appears to be day time now. Thomas and Mary are in shock, and have no idea what's going on. Once Mary hears the machine whistling in the distance, she immediately knows.)

Mary: "Alexander..."

(Everyone watches as a yellow mist flows out of the moonstone. It swirls through the air until it settles over a section of soldiers. Inside the mist appears a machine like creature. It starts off small, then grows larger. It continues to grow in the air until the legs are able to reach the ground. As they do, a few soldiers are squished underneath. Others try to back away in fear. The machine keeps increasing in size, until it is nearly half as tall as the castle. Even Nichols is amazed by the sight.)

Nichols: "I can't believe you've been keeping this secret from me the whole time."

(Once Alexander reaches full size, he looks around at the army before him. He opens up his mouth, and a yellow light starts to swirl around inside. The light grows so bright that everyone has to cover their eyes. A powerful blast of holy magic erupts from inside of him, and hits most of the Stephis army, Nichols included. The ground shakes with the impact, while dirt and rocks fly into the air. Half the Stephis army immediately falls, along with a chunk of the castle.)

Thomas: "Whoa!"

Mary: "Now's our chance!"

(Thomas and Mary quickly revive the rest of the group. They don't waste any time, but pick up their treasure sacks, and escape through the newly made space surrounding them. As the sun begins to appear in the sky, the army stands there in shock at what just happened. The party makes their way to the woods, and doesn't look back. The remaining army watches them leave, but nobody dares to follow them. Alexander himself slowly disintegrates into a yellow mist, and returns to the moonstone from where he came.)

Scene 6: The Shore

(Setting: On the shore to the north of Stephis. It is a bright and sunny day, and the now complete party is walking along the beach with Bart. They are making their way back to the Nautilus, which can be seen anchored out in the ocean. Each person is carrying a treasure sack as they go. The waves are crashing into the sand as they search for the boats they left here days ago. Scene begins with everyone talking.)

Amanda: "I still can't believe I missed all that. I would give anything to see the look on his face when Nichols saw Alexander blasting him away. He was aiming for him, right?"

Mary: "I think so. It was a lot to take in actually. I still can't believe what happened."

Bart: "Does this sort of thing happen to you guys often?"

Dustin: "You have no idea."

Thomas: "Alexander saved us. If it wasn't for him, we wouldn't be alive right now. Where did he even come from?"

Mary: (Grabs her necklace.) "He lives inside this stone. I've had it my whole life, and I don't even remember a time when I was without it. Doctor Tot used to teach me about Eidolons. He said that they will always come to your aid at your darkest hour."

Amanda: "It wiped out half the army though! That's some power!"

Mary: "I'm afraid I don't know much about them though. Tot had set out on a mission to find one particular Eidolon, but he was caught before he could get there. He did find another though." (Mary points to the diamond bracer on Cid's arm.)

Cid: (Lifts up his arm.) "You mean this has one of those creatures living inside?"

Mary: "Yes. That's why I need you to keep it safe. The Eidolon of thunder lives inside. Ramuh."

Amanda: "How come he didn't come out, and blow them all away?"

Mary: "I don't know. There is much I don't know actually. But what I do know is that I must continue the work that Doctor Tot started. I have to find Bahamut. He can help us defeat Stephis, once and for all. But I don't think I can do it alone. I will need some help."

Amanda: "I will help you."

Cid: "Me too."

Dustin: "Me three."

(Everyone looks at Thomas.)

Amanda: "Ehem."

Thomas: "I promise I will follow you to the ends of the earth. If this is what you must do, then I will be right there with you."

Amanda: "Yay! Way to go team!"

Dustin: (Looks at Bart.) "Any chance you are up for joining us?"

Bart: (Thinks.) "Hmmm. Your offer may be tempting, but I'm afraid I must decline. I shall restore my treasure, rebuild my crew, and set sail once again!"

Mary: "Have you not learned anything at all from this? Have you not yet chosen a side?"

Bart: "My lady, I have indeed learned much more than I ever thought possible. Fighting alongside you guys has taught me many things. And you have given me a lot to think about."

Thomas: "So what will you do now? Will you help us?"

Bart: "Help me take this treasure back to my ship, and let me take you to your next destination. I need some time to rebuild my crew. As you can see I am the only survivor. After that, if you should require my services, you know where to find me."

Amanda: "Now that's what I'm talking about!"

Cid: "Arrr! It's a pirate's life for me!"

(Everyone stops, and turns to look at Cid.)

Cid: (Shrugs.) "What I say?"

To be continued...

FFTP: Invasion

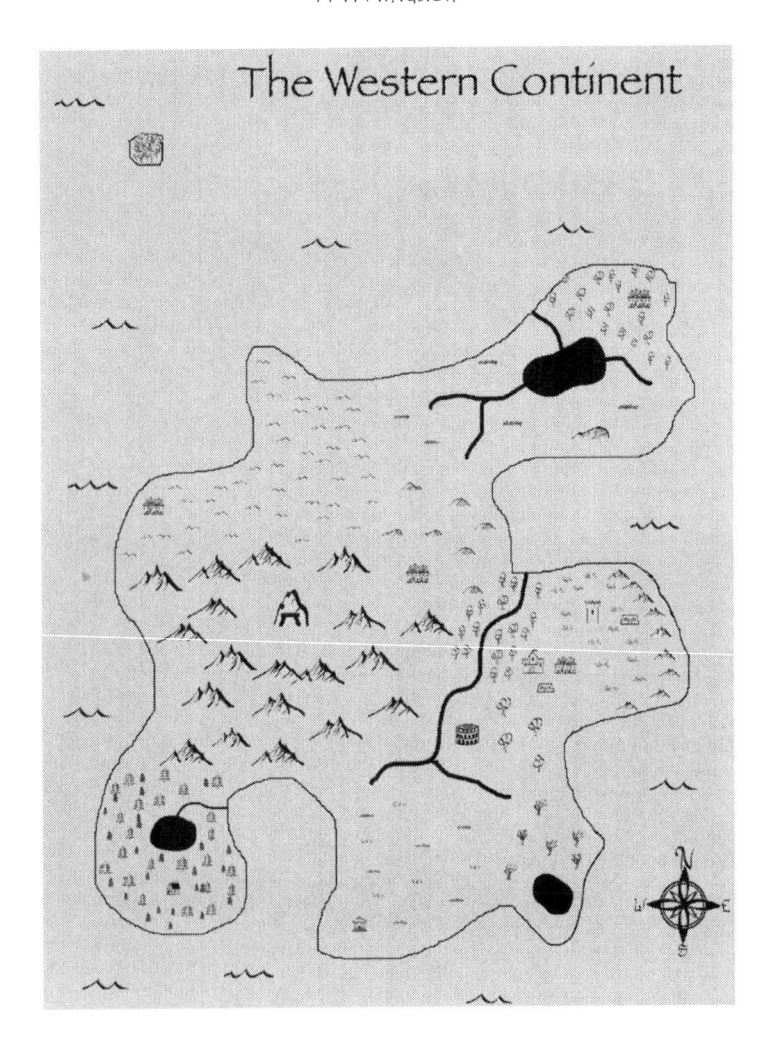

The Western Continent

The Eastern Continent

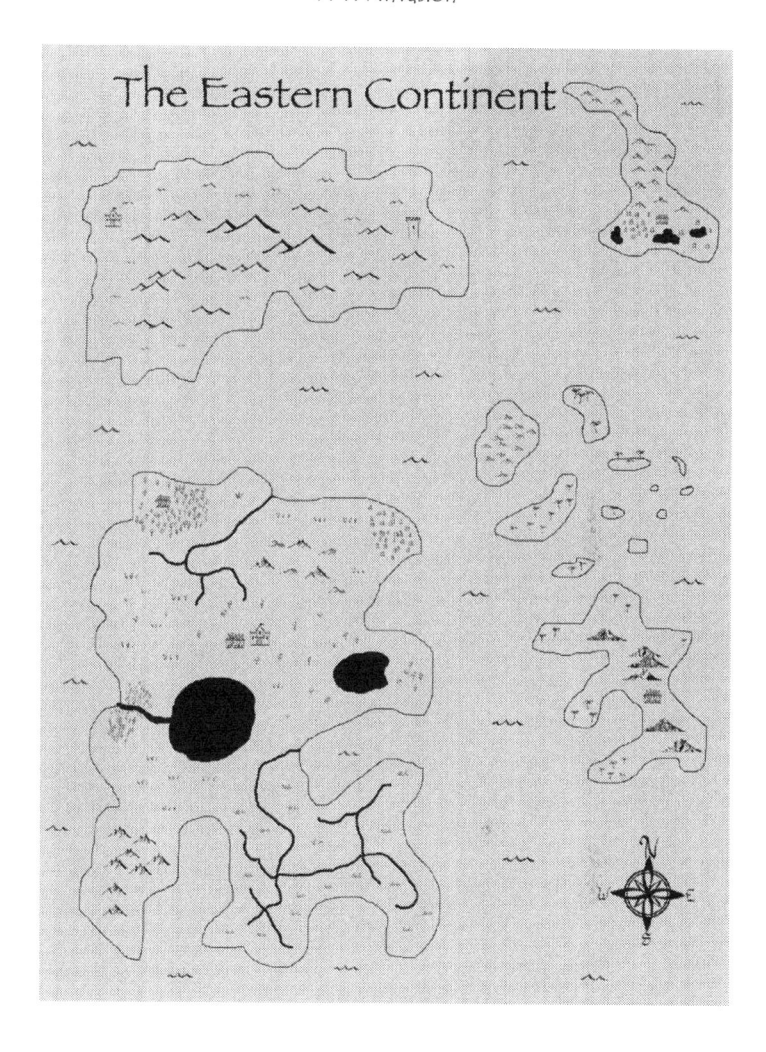

ABOUT THE AUTHOR

Thomas Edward Emmett Jr lives in a small town in NC. He currently works as a nurse, and as a group fitness instructor. He has been writing for most of his life, and has published a few books already. Besides work, he is finishing up his fifth degree. In his free time he enjoys writing, playing video games, fixing his house, and spending time in the mountains.

Made in the USA
Columbia, SC
09 January 2025